ANSWER TO PICTURE WRITING

I leave home. I go in my canoe on a journey to be gone five days. I arrive on an island. One family lives there. I meet a brave. We go to the woods. We hunt with bows and arrows. We kill a bear. We go in my canoe. We kill beavers. I start my return journey. After five days, I arrive home.

Legends of Green Sky Hill

LEGENDS OF
Green Sky Hill

told by
Louise Jean Walker

illustrated by
GRACE HOYT

published by
WM. B. EERDMANS, GRAND RAPIDS, MICHIGAN

In memory of my father

QUINTON SMITH WALKER

for his understanding, encouragement, and inspiration,
this volume is affectionately dedicated.

Foreword

A collection of Chippewa legends for the enjoyment of both juveniles and their elders was long overdue. The Michigan Chippewas have been known as storytellers ever since Henry Schoolcraft mistook Manabozho for Hiawatha. Now Louise Jean Walker is presenting a book of these Indian legends.

Children will like these stories. Parents can prove that popularity by reading them at the children's hour. Miss Walker herself has told them to hundreds of growing Americans; she knows how they rate with the young.

How do we happen to have the lovely trailing arbutus? How did the redman get his staff of life that we still call Indian corn? How did the original American ever learn from which tree to get his sugar? We all love butterflies; but why do we have to have mosquitoes? The Chippewa Indians have the answers, and Miss Walker gives them to us.

What the author calls THE ANIMAL PARADE has tales that compare favorably with like stories from Europe. The coyote stories of the Western tribes are not here because the Michigan of these tales had no coyotes. But do you know "Why the Cat Always Falls upon Her Feet," "Why the Rabbit Has Long Ears," "How the Snake Got Its Rattles," "How Beaver Fooled the Porcupines"? Read THE LEGENDS OF GREEN SKY HILL.

We can meet Manabozho and Peepuckewis and Glooskap and Laughing Eyes and the Indian Sandman on Green Sky Hill. Wait until I put on my Chippewa headdress and we will go together to Green Sky Hill and enjoy the legends.

—E. C. BECK

Ne-Gaun-Bi-A (He-Sits-Ahead)

Stillman College
Tuscaloosa, Alabama

Central Michigan University
Mt. Pleasant, Michigan

5

Dear Boys and Girls,

Here are some stories for you. They were told to me by a race known as American Indians. They inhabited our country before the Europeans came here. The Indians were composed of various families or tribes. They were alike in general appearance but spoke different tongues. Most of these tribes were usually at war with one another. They lived for the most part by hunting and fishing. While they had no marked boundaries, such as we have today, each tribe generally occupied a certain definite territory until driven out by some stronger force.

The men were tall and erect with skin of brown or bronze color. Their cheek bones were high, eyes piercing and dark, and their foreheads were inclined to slope backward. Their hair was coarse, straight and black. Some of them shaved their heads leaving only the scalp lock near the center. This was ornamented with the feather of an eagle, a hawk, a crow, or another bird that happened to be the favorite of the wearer. All the braves or nearly all kept their faces clean shaven. They wore little clothing. That which they wore consisted of leggings, blankets, and tunics made from the skins of animals or the feathers of birds.

The men found delight in hunting which extended through the trackless forest for a hundred miles. They enjoyed a feast which might last for several days.

The young women were slender, and lively, but, like all savage races, they lost the freshness and beauty of youth at an early age. They married young. As women, they performed the household tasks, planted and cared for the garden, skinned and dressed the meat, and preserved the food. They made the clothing and moccasins for their husbands and children with honest pride in their skill. As old women, they became the historians of their tribes. Trained to do this, every one of them could sit at some council and repeat every word that was said and describe every act, years afterward with remarkable accuracy.

Indians were a religious people. They believed in many gods and spirits; but no one of these is a Great Spirit in the sense in which we use the term. However, every tribe had some legend of a creator or first maker to whom the tribe owed its origin. He was a combination of strength, weakness, wisdom, folly, kindness, and malice.

The Indian had an interesting story for every act of his daily life. It didn't matter whether he sang, danced, prayed, hunted, built a fire, or went to war. These stories are called legends. Many of them are about stars, mountains, trees, animals, flowers, birds and plants, for the Indians were the ideal children of nature. Without a written language themselves except that of symbols, rude signs, and pictures, much of the Indian's story could not be told. Yet every rock, river, lake, mountain or valley recalled to the Indians some deed of valor, incident of love, or remembrance of wrong. These memories lived in stories that were told to each succeeding generation. They were told with lowered voice and an air of mystery.

Many of the Indians today are forgetting or have forgotten these ancient stories. But in the old days, it was a sacred duty to deliver the stories from one generation to another. Indian children had no schoolbooks. From the legends, they learned many of nature's secrets and the history of their people. The old men felt pride in their knowledge of these legends. They tried to hand them down in the exact form in which they had received them. It was customary for the old Indian Chief to tell these legends to the sons or daughters who showed the most ability.

I hope that you will enjoy these stories.

LOUISE JEAN WALKER

CONTENTS

The Fairest Flowers o' the Season

One

OLD MAN WINTER

In a cabin in a dark forest, there once lived a very lonely, old man whose name was Old Man Winter. He had very few friends, even among the birds and the animals. During an unusually severe winter, the old man suffered with the bitter cold in spite of his warm bearskin clothing.

One day when a terrible snowstorm was raging and the air was icy and cut like a knife, the old man found that he could not leave his cabin, for a powerful wind had blown the snow in deep drifts six feet high before the door. The old man was greatly alarmed and panicky when he realized that he was snowbound. He became very sad. In his despair, he prayed to the Great Spirit, Manito, for help. At last, Manito heard the old man's prayers and sent the North Wind to blow open the cabin door. The North Wind blew loudly and fiercely for a long time. Finally, after a powerful gust, the door flew open, but by this time Old Man Winter, who was lying on the floor, was too weak to get up and close it.

In a short time, a tall and beautiful maiden entered the

cabin. On her head was a garland of fragrant, pink flowers which perfumed the air and made the whole room seem warm and pleasant. Her feet were clad with moccasins made of white lilies, and her gown was fashioned with lacy ferns, sweet grasses, leafy buds, and lovely blossoms.

Old Man Winter looked up at his young visitor with wonder for he felt that she had been sent by the Great Manito as an answer to his earnest prayer. He was sure that this lovely maiden must be powerful and gifted with magic like himself. Consequently, he welcomed her and then asked her name and why she had come to the cabin.

But the beautiful maiden only smiled.

Then Old Man Winter told her about his own magical power. He said, "I make the leaves turn red, yellow and brown. Later I cause them to dry and fall from the trees. When I give the command, the birds in great flocks hurry southward, and the animals seek shelter in caves and dens. With my icy breath, I freeze the rivers and lakes. Finally at my bidding, the snow comes and covers the forest, fields, and roads with deep drifts."

Then the beautiful visitor smiled at the old man again and said, "Now I shall tell you about my power. I bring the gentle rain and the warm sunshine; at my bidding, the leaves burst forth; spring beauties, mayflowers, anemones, violets, trillium and cowslips bloom; all the birds return from the South, and all the animals that have been hiding in caves during the cold winter awake from their sleep. The birds fill the woods with songs of joy and gladness. Then all the children are happy and gay. Everyone welcomes me, for I bring the pleasant weather."

Presently, Old Man Winter began to grow warm and very sleepy. At last, he just couldn't keep his eyes open any longer, for Manito felt that this old man had been powerful long enough and that the beautiful maiden should reign in his stead. Gradually her power caused the old man to grow very small and at last to fall into a deep sleep.

In a short time, the maiden laid on the ground vines of waxy green leaves and fragrant pink flowers like those that she wore in her hair. Then she stole away softly. Soon from every print of her moccasined feet there sprang more of the lovely trailing arbutus, a tribute to her magic which had caused sleep to overcome Old Man Winter. Even to this day, if one will go into the woods of Northern Michigan in March or April, he will find these lovely flowers, the heralds of Spring, hidden under last year's dry leaves and grass.

Two

THE STAR MAIDEN

The fairies loved the Chippewas. Their land was the home of many spirits, and as long as the Chippewas lived on the shores of the Great Lakes, the woods were full of fairies. Some of them lived in the trunks of the graceful, white birches; others dwelt in the moss at the roots or on the trunks of the silvery aspens. Some hid beneath the mushrooms and the toadstools; others concealed themselves in Jack-in-the-Pulpits, or under wild strawberry plants. Some fairies changed themselves into beautiful butterflies like the Black and Tiger Swallowtails and the Monarch or even tinier insects with shining wings. They transformed themselves thus that they might be near the children whom they loved and that they might play together in the bright sunshine.

Now unfortunately, there were also some very mischievous and evil spirits in the lands of the Chippewas. These bad spirits often burrowed into the ground and gnawed at the roots of the loveliest flowers and finest vegetables until they completely destroyed them. They often caused the corn to wither and die. The woods, the shores,

16

and all the bays and islands were the homes of these keen and mischievous spirits. They listened whenever they heard the Indians talking and carried the news and gossip to those to whom it would do the most mischief and harm. In the spring and summer, because of these bad spirits, the Indians had to be silent in the woods and could speak only in whispers. But when winter brought the deep snows and piled huge drifts around the wigwams, the evil spirits grew drowsy and were soon fast asleep under a blanket of snow.

All the Chippewas loved the good spirits and looked out for their interests. They never trampled on the flowers nor pulled the moss from the trees. They never disturbed the beautiful butterflies that rested on clumps of Queen Anne's Lace or on the Butterfly Weed.

The Chippewas, after their day's work was over, were accustomed to sit and smoke in the doorway of their wigwams and watch the brilliant rays of the setting sun. Then, when the light had faded into evening, they listened to the voices of the fairies and the hum of insects and the thousands of tiny noises that night always brings.

One summer night as they listened, they saw a very bright light shining in the top of the tallest tree. It was the brightest star in the sky and it appeared to be very near the earth. When the Indians went close to the tree, they found that the star was caught in the highest branch.

The Chippewas were perplexed and didn't know what to do. Finally, they summoned to a council all the aged men, for they were considered the wisest. For three nights, these aged Indians sat around the council fire, but they reached no decision about the star.

Finally, a young warrior came to them and said, "Last night, I had a dream and through it I found out about the star. While I was asleep, the West Wind blew back the

17

curtain of my wigwam and the light of the star fell upon my face. Presently, a beautiful maiden stood beside me. I was very much surprised and did not dare to speak lest she would disappear. She smiled down upon me and told me that her home was in the star. Then she said, 'In my wanderings over the whole earth, I have seen no land as beautiful as that of the Chippewas. Its flowers, its sweet-voiced birds, its beautiful lakes and rivers, its majestic trees, and its huge dunes of gleaming sand have charmed me so that I do not wish to wander any more. If your people will welcome me, I would like to make my home among you if you would show me a place where I could dwell.' "

The Wisemen were pleased with the young warrior's report. Immediately, they began discussing the best spot for the beautiful maiden's home. When the Council couldn't agree, the Wisemen decided that the maiden would have to choose for herself, but they offered several suggestions.

"Why not make your home in the tall cedar?" suggested one of the Wisemen. "Its boughs are strong and safe."

"No," replied the maiden. "There I would have only birds for my companions. I wish to be nearer the earth where I can meet the people whom I have learned to love."

"Perhaps you would like to dwell on a hillside," said another. "You could look down on all the activity about you." But the maiden shook her head. "No, I do not want to live there."

"Would you like to live in a green valley? It would be quiet and peaceful," suggested the most aged Indian. Again the maiden shook her head.

Finally she said, "I'm sorry, but not one of these places that you have suggested will do. I am afraid you cannot help me. I shall have to find a home for myself."

To do so did not prove an easy task. In fact, the beautiful

maiden was almost in despair; however, one day as she looked down from the edge of a tall rock overlooking a lake, she saw a white flower with a heart of gold shining on the waters below. As she looked, a canoe, steered by the young Warrior who had told her wishes to his people, shot past and the strong, brown hand brushed the edge of the flower.

"That is the home for me!" she exclaimed and half skipping, half flying down the side of the rock, she soon dropped into the water and hid herself in the bosom of the flower. There she realized that she could watch the stars, and talk to the star spirits who bathed in the clear lake; best of all, there she could watch the people whom she loved, for their canoes were always skimming over the lakes. From that day, even to the present time, she has continued to make her home in the Northern waters.

Three

FRINGED GENTIAN

Long ago, before the white men came to America, a beautiful Indian girl lived on the northern shore of the Straits of Mackinac. This maiden with long black braids was even lovelier than the beautiful flowers from which she received her name. Deep in the forest, fragrant with firs, pines, and wild flowers, was her wigwam home. Here Fringed Gentian spent a happy childhood.

When the snow lay upon the forests of the North, and ice covered the rivers and lakes, the storytellers of the Chippewas recited tales of long ago. Grouped with other eager listeners, Fringed Gentian sat through the long winters until the frogs began croaking in the spring, that she might hear about the prowess of her people. In the summertime, she wandered through the forests picking fringed gentians and sweet grasses. Often she rested on the bank of a stream in the shade of a pine or birch and watched fish leap and dart in the limpid water.

20

Happy and carefree, she grew into young womanhood. Soon many young braves admired Fringed Gentian's beautiful form, raven-like hair and winning smile. At length, a handsome young warrior named White Feather came to woo her. As a wrestler and hunter, no other brave could match his skill. Many other Indian maidens hoped to become his wife, but he admired only Fringed Gentian. Soon they fell in love.

One day when White Feather was hunting in the forest, he met an old warrior named Black Hawk.

"Good morning, White Feather," said the aged Indian. "You should be hunting for a wife rather than for game."

"That advice comes too late, O Wise One, for I have already found her. She is the loveliest of all the maidens; her voice is full of music and laughter; few can excel her in weaving. Today I am going to ask her father to let me marry her and take her to my wigwam."

"May your luck never change," answered Black Hawk as he continued on his way.

In the afternoon when Fringed Gentian returned to her home after one of her long rambles, she saw that a stranger had come during her absence. In front of the wigwam sat a very old chief engaged in serious conversation with her father. The two talked long and earnestly. Nearby lay skins of the bear, the buck, and the fox, and strips of hide which he had brought with him. As Fringed Gentian paused before withdrawing, as was the custom when her elders talked, she heard the old chief say, "Because we have been friends, I want your daughter for my wigwam. I am bringing you these gifts in exchange for her. They are the finest of the forest."

Fringed Gentian's father shook his head. "No, Black Hawk, they are not enough. My daughter has many ad-

mirers who would pay me more than you have offered. She is no ordinary maiden."

Black Hawk remained silent. At length, he said gruffly, "You are much too demanding for a friend, but I will give you five more beaver- and two more bearskins for the woman." Fringed Gentian's father still refused. As the young girl rested on the log, she noticed Black Hawk watching her greedily as he continued to smoke. Then he laid more gifts before Fringed Gentian's father. This time he offered knives, beads, tobacco, and blankets. These made the father's eyes glitter. At length, he said, "You have made a shrewd bargain, Black Hawk. In a few days, I shall let you have my daughter."

In the meantime, White Feather's light and hasty step brought him to the clearing near Fringed Gentian's home. As he approached, White Feather was so surprised to see Fringed Gentian seated nearby on a log and weeping bitterly that his feet lost their noiseless step and he tripped on a stick. This commotion caused Fringed Gentian to glance up. Recognizing her lover, she ran quickly to him. Black Hawk and Fringed Gentian's father watched as she clung to the young warrior. "Oh, White Feather, you have come, too," she sobbed.

"Yes, my love, I have come to gain your father's permission to marry you and to claim you for my own. Why do I find you weeping?"

Before Fringed Gentian could tell him of the unwelcome suitor's proposal, Black Hawk said arrogantly, "Is this the home of your sweetheart, White Feather?"

"Yes, Brave One," answered the youth.

Then Fringed Gentian's father stepped forward and said, "You are too late, young warrior. I have given my daughter to my friend, Black Hawk. She will be his woman hereafter."

Black Hawk walked away proudly toward his home.

Tears streamed down Fringed Gentian's face as she watched White Feather disappear into the woods. For hours, she wept silently.

Her father watched her and continued to smoke. After a while, he said, "My daughter, do not weep. White Feather may be handsome, but he has no rich gifts to offer. Black Hawk shall be your husband. He is a rich and a wise trader. You shall have comfort in his wigwam."

Fringed Gentian remained silent, for her heart belonged to White Feather. When she realized that her father was determined to have her marry the old trader, she soon lost her gay spirit. She spent hours wandering through the woods. At mealtime, she barely touched her food. She was listless.

Soon her mother started the preparations for the wedding. First of all, clothing, moccasins, rugs, and blankets were made for Fringed Gentian to take to her new home. Later, under the savory kettles, fire burned; meats were roasted, and meal was prepared for bread. During all these preparations, Fringed Gentian continued sorrowful and depressed. The thought of her wedding day only made her miserable.

One day she went to her grandmother's wigwam and told the aged woman of her unhappiness and heartache. "O Grandmother, I would rather die than be Black Hawk's wife! He wants a strong, young woman to be his slave. I hate the ugly old man. What can I do?"

Grandmother smoked her pipe and meditated. After she had thought for some time, stroking Fringed Gentian's hair, she said, "Be brave, my child. Your trouble shall be mine hereafter. Only be at the big rock at sunup on your wedding day."

"Yes, Grandmother," answered Fringed Gentian. With a lighter heart, the girl left her grandmother's home, trusting in the old squaw's words, "Your trouble shall be mine hereafter."

Soon after Fringed Gentian's departure, the old grandmother sent a brave to White Feather to ask him to come to her.

In a short time, White Feather's face appeared in the fire light in front of the wigwam.

"You sent for me?" inquired the youth.

"Yes, White Feather, I did," said the old squaw. "Fringed Gentian came today to my wigwam brokenhearted because her father has promised her to Black Hawk. Her heart is yours."

"I love her very much," he answered sadly. "I had hoped we could wed, but it seems that Black Hawk has more to offer."

"Even though Black Hawk is a rich trader he cannot buy Fringed Gentian's love. Do not give her up so easily! She will be yours if you will carry out my plan," promised the aged woman.

"What plan?" asked the youth, as a smile encircled his face.

"Meet her at the big rock at sunup on the day of her wedding. You can run away together," the grandmother answered. "I'll let you know the day she is to be married."

"Do you think Fringed Gentian would dare to do that?" he inquired.

"I am sure she would," the grandmother answered. "She will be at the big rock at sunup. You and I must make some preparations."

"How can I thank you!" exclaimed White Feather happily.

"Don't thank me," she answered gravely. "Thank the lucky star under which you walked tonight, and may the Great Spirit keep watch over you, my son."

On her wedding day, while the sky was still dark and dappled here and there with spots of gray, Fringed Gentian hurried away from her father's wigwam. After a short walk, she reached the top of the big rock overlooking the lake which seemed as friendly and as blue as the beautiful flowers. Suddenly, she leaped from this great rock into the deep water far below. As she dropped from the great height,

25

White Feather caught her in his strong arms and swam with her to his canoe, hidden in the shadow of the rocks.

Standing in the early morning sunshine on the summit of the rock, Fringed Gentian's grandmother waved her hand in blessing to the happy pair.

They paddled to Saint Helena where White Feather and Fringed Gentian's grandmother had already furnished the wigwam. Fringed Gentian and White Feather were married and settled comfortably in their own home.

At last, Fringed Gentian was truly happy as a lovely maiden should be. Often she walked the trails through the pines and fir trees to meet her husband when he returned from a hunting trip. Some of the beauty of her former home had come with her. On her beaded moccasins clung hundreds of tiny seeds of the beautiful blue gentians that had grown around her father's wigwam. These seeds fell into the friendly soil of Saint Helena where they took root and grew into lovely blue flowers. They made this beautiful spot their home, too. In fact, the flowers liked Saint Helena so much that they grow there in profusion even today.

Four

WHY ROSES HAVE THORNS

Long ago, roses of every color grew abundantly. The stems and branches of the rosebush were smooth and fragrant. Would you believe it, there were no thorns nor briars on the bushes! Everyone loved the roses and picked them freely. Not only the people liked them, but also all the animals that ate grass or browsed, eagerly sought for these beautiful flowers, and ate the fragrant blooms and the bushes. In fact, they liked them so much that before very long there was grave danger that all the roses would be destroyed and there would be no more.

In those days, trees and flowers had a great and unusual power which they do not possess today. They could think and act. When the flowers realized that the roses were nearly all gone, they called a council to decide how to preserve the few that were left. All kinds of roses came to this meeting and soon each one told how its life was constantly in danger. Finally, the Council decided to send a committee of roses to talk over the trouble with Manabozho. He seemed to be the only person who could help them.

27

Now although Manabozho was a friend of the Indians, he was a queer fellow. He could change himself into any animal that he wished and often he took the form of a rabbit. Because he could assume many different shapes, the Committee had trouble finding him. On this long journey, they often stopped the animals that they met to inquire about Manabozho's whereabouts. They even asked the trees and the hills. Finally, a tree said to them, "Manabozho is living in a valley among the mountains. He is busy raising a garden."

Encouraged by this news, the roses hurried to his home as fast as the fierce wind which they had hired could blow them along.

When the Committee reached the spot where Manabozho lived, they were frightened. They didn't know just how to approach Manabozho. While they were waiting to get up their courage, they heard loud, angry tones. Some of the company recognized them as Manabozho's voice. Evidently, he was very angry. They became even more afraid to go into his presence! However, they had come too far to be discouraged and to give up their plan. One of the group suggested that the Committee hide behind a row of balsam trees and try to find out the reason for Manabozho's anger. The rest agreed that the idea was a good one.

At this time, Manabozho was very much interested in his garden. He had planted beans, corn, squash, and pumpkin. All the vegetables grew so well and looked so flourishing that Manabozho was proud of his efforts.

In order to protect the vegetables from prowling wild animals, he had planted a hedge of beautiful rose bushes around the edge of the garden. Manabozho had worked hard to make the hedge. He had transplanted some of the roses from great distances because these flowers didn't grow

near his home, and besides, they were not so abundant as in former times.

Just before the arrival of the Committee, Manabozho had returned from one of his trips. He hurried to see how the garden had grown while he was gone. Alas, all kinds of animals, ranging from the rabbit to the deer, had visited Manabozho's home in his absence! They had eaten the rose hedge and spoiled his whole garden. No wonder he was angry!

As soon as the Committee knew the cause of Manabozho's anger, they hurried to him. The sight of them

29

excited his curiosity, for he had believed that all the rose bushes were dead.

Then one of the company acted as a spokesman and said, "O Manabozho, please come to our assistance and save us from being destroyed by our enemies. Only a few of us have survived." The rest of the roses added their pleas for Manabozho's help.

When Manabozho had heard all about the troubles of the roses, he exclaimed, "This is a very perplexing problem. Leave me for a few hours, that I may think of a solution. Come back before sunset." The roses hurriedly left Manabozho's presence. Just before sunset, they returned.

When they had gathered in his presence, he said, "Beautiful flowers, I have decided to cover every inch of your stems and branches with thornlike prickers so that every animal henceforth will be afraid to touch you."

The roses were delighted with this form of protection. They felt sure that they would be saved.

Because of Manabozho's help and his clever plan, many kinds of roses grow in the gardens of the world today.

Hidden Treasures

Five

THE ORIGIN OF INDIAN CORN

Long, long ago, Watoge, a poor Indian, together with his wife and children, lived in a rude wigwam on a broad plain. Although the country was beautiful, there were no lakes and woods near their home. Consequently, since Watoge had little chance to hunt and fish, he often had trouble finding food for his family. Many times, his children were hungry. Although Watoge was poor, he was kind to strangers and was always thankful to the Great Spirit for everything which he received. The family desired above all else to please the Great Spirit.

When the oldest son, Yoome, reached his twelfth birthday, his parents prepared him for a fast. At that age, the young braves of the tribe were accustomed to spend some time alone in meditation and in communion with the Great Spirit, that they might be able to take up the responsibilities of manhood seriously. Yoome was eager to find out what kind of spirit would be his guide throughout his life.

His parents built a little lodge for him not far from their wigwam, where he was to stay during the days of his fast.

33

Then one morning, Watoge took Yoome to the lodge. After the father had counselled his son and given him his blessing, he returned home. During the first few days, Yoome wandered across the broad plain. He wanted to know how the plants, berries, and birds grew. He wondered why some plants were suitable for food and others were used for medicine. He knew that some plants were full of poison. Yoome remembered that the Great Spirit created all things and that he was all powerful. As the young brave walked alone, he wondered whether the Great Spirit would help the Indians get some food other than by hunting animals and catching fish. Day after day as he fasted, he thought, "I must do something to help my people." This desire was uppermost in his mind and he prayed fervently to the Great Spirit for guidance and direction.

After Yoome had fasted three days, he felt too weak to rise. He lay on the bearskin and rested throughout the day. When Yoome fell asleep, he dreamed that he saw a handsome, young man come down from the sky and walk toward him. This stranger with graceful bearing was beautifully dressed and wore many garments of different shades of green and yellow. His head was crowned with waving feathers.

When the young man approached Yoome, he said, "I am a messenger sent to you by the Great Spirit who made all things. He has seen you fasting and knows that you wish to assist your people. Since you do not seek strength for war, or praise from warriors, the Great Spirit has sent me to instruct you and help you." Then the stranger commanded Yoome to rise and wrestle valiantly with him. Yoome felt very weak and inadequate, for he hadn't eaten for several days. Nevertheless, he arose, for he was determined not to fail in his duty. After they had wrestled for a while, the stranger said, "That is enough for now, but I shall come again to try you." Then he left and disappeared into the air.

The next day, when the visitor came again, he started wrestling with Yoome whose strength was even less than it had been the day before. Yet his courage was greater even though his strength was less. After wrestling, the visitor again spoke and said, "Tomorrow on your last trial be strong, for that is the only way you can conquer and obtain your wish." On the third day, when the visitor arrived, Yoome was still weaker; however, he was determined to win or die in the effort. After he had wrestled bravely for some time, the stranger stopped and said, "You have conquered me."

Then the visitor followed Yoome into the lodge and sat down beside him. Turning to him, the visitor said, "You have won your wish from the Great Spirit, for you have wrestled bravely. Tomorrow will be the seventh day of your fasting. On that day, your father will bring you food. When we wrestle for the last time, you will be the victor. Therefore, listen carefully now to my words, that you may learn what to do to assist your family, and your tribe. As soon as we wrestle tomorrow and you win, you must strip off my garments, throw me down and then clear away the roots and weeds and bury me on this spot. After you have performed these tasks, leave my body in the earth, but come back after a few days to see whether I have come to life. Throughout the spring, be careful to keep the grass and weeds away from my grave. If you obey my instructions, you will help your people and you can teach them what I have taught you." Then the friends shook hands, and the Spirit's messenger departed.

Next day, when Watoge arrived with some food for his

son, he urged Yoome to eat, since he had been fasting for seven days. Though the food looked tempting, Yoome wanted to fast a few hours longer; the father consented to his son's wish and left for home.

A little while later the friendly visitor returned. Although Yoome had not eaten anything, yet he felt strong and brave. He wrestled with the visitor and soon hurled him to the ground. Then he removed the visitor's beautiful garments and plume. Finding his friend dead, he buried him at once and obeyed every command carefully. Somehow he felt confident that his friend would again come to life.

When Yoome returned home, he ate the food which his mother had prepared. Later, he kept busy doing the tasks that his father assigned to him each day. But he never for a moment forgot the grave of this visitor, and he visited it throughout the spring and early summer. He pulled out the weeds, kept the earth soft, and very soon, he noticed the tops of the green plumes coming through the ground. The more carefully he tended the ground to keep it soft and clean, the faster the plumes seemed to grow. Yoome was careful not to let his father know about the grave.

One day, when the summer was nearly over, Yoome decided to revisit the place where he had fasted. He invited his father to go with him. The lodge was gone, but in its place stood a tall plant with bright, colored, silken hair, topped with nodding plumes and beautiful leaves and golden clusters on each side. "It is my friend!" shouted Yoome. "It is corn, the friend of all men. Hereafter, we shall not have so much trouble in securing food, and we shall not have to depend on hunting entirely. As long as we take care of this gift, the ground will give us a living." Then Yoome, pulling off one ear, said, "See, Father, this is what I asked for when I fasted. The Great Spirit heard my

prayer and sent us something new, and now our people will not need to depend entirely upon fish and meat for their food."

Yoome then told his father all the instructions which he had received from the stranger and showed him how to tear away the broad husks. As soon as they reached their home, they built a fire and held the ears over the red coals till the outer skin became brown. Then the family feasted on the delicious food and thanked the Great Spirit for his gift which he had sent into the world and which has since proved to be a blessing to all men.

Six

THE FORTUNATE MISTAKE

"Today I am going to the woods to shoot squirrels. While I am gone, cook the venison. I want a good supper all ready when I get back," said Chief Shawondasee. Then, picking up his club and his bow and arrows, he left the bark-covered wigwam.

From the doorway Wenonah watched her tall, stalwart husband as he walked toward the woods. She was proud of the eagle feathers which he wore in his black hair and the figure of the beaver painted on his naked chest. As soon as he was out of sight, his wife quickly picked up the bedding and laid it on the bushes and poles to air. She swept the earth around the fire with her grass broom.

When she had finished her morning work and had folded the blankets, Wenonah began to feel lonely. The early March day seemed very dreary. All she could hear was the whistling of the wind and the flapping of the skins on the wigwam door. "Guess I'd better start to make a blanket," she said to herself. She took some dry rabbit skins from the frames and cut the skins into strips and sewed the ends together. But after a while she grew restless and tired of this work. She left her place by the fire and went to the door. The sun was peeping through the gray clouds. Then she said, half-aloud, "Maybe the day isn't going to be too bad. Why don't I go to see Laughing Flower? I haven't seen her in a long time." She decided to set out at once.

When the young wife reached Laughing Flower's home, she found two other squaws there. The time passed very quickly as the four women laughed, gossiped and wove beaded bands for their hair.

In fact, Wenonah was enjoying herself so much that the sun had long passed over her head before she remembered that her husband would be returning soon. When she recalled his words about a good supper, she hurried home as rapidly as she could run. On her arrival she quickly rekindled the fire and started to put the venison in the pot, but when she reached for the elk-hide water bag to fill the pot, she discovered that the bag was empty. Wenonah realized that she didn't have time to go for water, for the river was a long distance from the wigwam. "What shall I do? How can I prepare the venison?" she cried.

Wenonah was frightened. She trembled when she thought how angry Chief Shawondasee would be if a venison supper was not ready for him. "Possibly Chibiabos can help me," she exclaimed. As soon as the thought came to her, Wenonah sped through the forest like a deer to see the aged Chibiabos, her husband's mother. "Only Chibiabos, the Wise One, can tell me what to do," she kept repeating as she ran toward the wigwam.

When Chibiabos heard from Wenonah's own lips about her carelessness, the Aged One shook her head sadly. "To be like the cuckoo bird does not become the wife of the

Great Chief Shawondasee," she spoke solemnly. "Return quickly to your fire and cook your master's supper."

"But I have no water!" Wenonah sobbed.

The old woman turned her back upon the weeping Wenonah and stared into the fire. "The wife of Shawondasee must find water," she answered slowly.

Wenonah bowed low, then picked up her bucket and the empty water bag. She understood that the Wise One would not help her, and that by her own efforts she must find water to cook the venison, for that was the duty of the wife of a great Indian chief. Chibiabos had made that fact plain to her daughter-in-law.

However, Wenonah did not feel capable and efficient like the wife of a great chief. She remembered that Shawondasee had scolded her several times previously for her negligence. She was very unhappy and frightened; in fact, she was so very much discouraged and distracted that she stopped running and threw herself, exhausted and sobbing, at the foot of a tall maple tree. As she lay there, trying to decide what she should do, she felt something fall on her hand like drops of rain. Soon she saw it was water trickling down the trunk of the tree! It was dripping steadily from the fresh cut which some brave had put in the tree for a trail marker. Wenonah raised thankful eyes toward the heavens to the Great Spirit who had heard her prayers and had sent water up from the very heart of the big maple tree. Now the great chief need not go hungry!

Quickly the young wife peeled a piece of bark from a stick, put it in the gash for a spout, and placed the bucket beneath the cut. After a short time, she had sufficient water for the venison and so she hurried home to cook it. The contents of the pot were soon bubbling merrily and a pleasant odor filled the wigwam.

When it was about time for Shawondasee to return home, Wenonah lifted the lid and peeped into the kettle to look at the stew. Something was wrong! The water in the kettle had practically boiled away; the venison and the inside of the kettle were coated with tiny brown crystals. Arising from the kettle was a strange sweet odor; in fact, it was one which Wenonah had never smelled before. Immediately fear seized her. She exclaimed, "I've spoiled the venison! Now the chief will be angry, very angry. What can I do? Where shall I go?" Panic-stricken, she hurried from the wigwam to hide in the forest.

Wenonah, wandering about in the woods, wept bitterly because of her carelessness. She reminded herself that she was not fit to be the wife of a great chief for she had failed again. "Yes, Chibiabos was quite right," she admitted to herself. "I am like the cuckoo bird and not worthy to be the wife of a great chief for he is like a great eagle."

41

In the meantime, Chief Shawondasee returned home and wondered where his wife had gone. He smelled the venison cooking and went straight to the pot. Immediately, he sat down to enjoy his supper.

Wenonah stayed in the woods until it was nearly dark. She became very hungry and decided she must tell Chief Shawondasee what she had done. Sick with fear, she started slowly toward her home, for she knew her husband would punish her. Trembling and scarcely daring to breathe, she crept close to the wigwam and peeped inside. There sat Shawondasee dipping his fingers into the kettle, licking the sticky liquid from them, and grunting each time he tasted the syrup. He looked very contented. Soon he had eaten all the venison and the sugary crystals clinging to the sides of the kettle. He continued to dip his fingers into the pot and lick them with great relish. Puzzled, Wenonah slipped through the door of the wigwam to her husband's side and, unnoticed, watched him curiously. At length, when Shawondasee, looking up, saw Wenonah, he said, "You taste. Um! Good! Where did you get this?"

Wenonah dipped her fingers into the kettle and then put them into her mouth. That minute she realized why her husband was not angry. The syrup on her fingers was delicious; in fact, she had never tasted anything so good before. The chief and his wife scraped every particle of sugar from the kettle. Then Wenonah told her husband the whole story.

Chief Shawondasee was so pleased with the syrup that every spring he ordered all the braves to catch the sap from the maple trees, and the squaws to boil it down into sugar. During the winter, the squaws would thoroughly clean the bills of the ducks which they had killed for food and save the little bonelike casings. Each spring, after they had boiled the sap sufficiently, the squaws would pour the thick, hot syrup into these little containers. When the syrup had cooled and hardened, the Indian children ate these lumps of maple sugar. It was the first candy that they ever tasted.

Seven

HOW THE INDIANS RECEIVED TOBACCO

Very many winters ago, Manabozho decided to make another one of his long journeys. After walking for many moons, he came to a land of high mountains with lofty peaks. This rugged country was new and strange to the magician. He was pleased with the unusual sights and said to himself, "Here I shall stop for a while. I need a rest from all responsibility. For years, I have borne the troubles of the Indians and have settled their difficulties. Now I must think of myself." Therefore, Manabozho settled down for some time in a valley nestled among the mountains in this pleasant country. At first he wandered about in the foothills, but later became so familiar with the region that he climbed to the summit of the highest peaks.

One day, when he passed through a gap between the peaks, he saw some blue smoke slowly coming out of a chasm. This sight aroused his curiosity; consequently, he hurried to see who was causing it and to find out what was burning. As he drew near the chasm, he smelled a peculiar but pleasing odor.

As Manabozho made his way into the cave, the odor grew stronger. In the semi-darkness, he bumped against great bales and bags. They were so many that Manabozho found it difficult to get around in this narrow passage, but finally, after slowly and carefully picking his way, the magician reached the center of the smoke-filled cavern. Imagine his surprise and terror! A huge giant, the largest person he had ever seen, lay asleep among great bales and bags of tobacco. Scores of pipes and ashes lay near his side.

Unfortunately, Manabozho's stumbling around in the smoke and darkness had disturbed the lumpish giant, and caused him to wake up. When he saw Manabozho, he roared, "What do you want here? Get out! Nobody in the world dares to disturb my sleep."

Manabozho, still a bit frightened, said, "Oh, I am sorry I awakened you. Please may I have some of the stuff that smells so fragrant? I am pleased with its odor."

The giant, still impatient with Manabozho, replied surlily, "No, you can't have a single bit. I give portions away to only a few friends who come here every year to smoke with me. Get out and leave me alone!"

When Manabozho realized that he was not going to get any tobacco by pleading, he snatched one of the well-filled bags, dashed out of the cave, and ran as rapidly as possible.

The enormous giant in a terrible rage pursued rash Manabozho who had stolen the tobacco from under his very nose. In that desperate race, Manabozho was forced to jump from one mountain top to the next one and from peak to peak while close behind him paced the giant in hot pursuit. The earth seemed to shake under the tread of his feet. Manabozho had to run for his life as they raced neck and neck.

Fortunately, by this time Manabozho was well acquainted with the mountains of the region and remembered that the one ahead of him had a very steep cliff on the other side.

"Oh, if I could only reach the top!" Manabozho thought. Since he had no choice, he started to climb to the summit. The big, clumsy giant attempted to follow and was soon panting for breath. However, he had an advantage in that he could take longer strides than Manabozho. When the magician reached the summit, he suddenly threw himself face downward at the very edge of the peak, but the giant running at such a high rate of speed couldn't stop so abruptly. When he passed over Manabozho, the latter gave the giant such a hard push that he fell over the steep cliff and into the valley below.

The giant was badly bruised and wounded. As soon as

he managed to rise, he started limping away down the valley. Manabozho saw that the giant looked like a giant grasshopper. He burst out laughing and cried gleefully, "For your meanness and selfishness, I shall change you into a great grasshopper. You shall always have a dirty mouth and appear to be chewing tobacco."

When Manabozho was rested, he returned to the giant's cave and took possession of the great quantities of tobacco that he found there. He divided it among the Indian tribes. Since that time, those who live where tobacco will grow have cultivated it and have supplied others with it.

Eight

THE FIRST STRAWBERRIES

After the first man and woman were created they lived happily for a time. Then they began to quarrel. Soon they were quarreling often.

Life in the wigwam became so unpleasant that the squaw decided to leave her husband and her home. She started toward the land of the setting sun.

After the wife had been gone a little while, the wigwam seemed very quiet. The husband grew lonesome. He sat down in front of the campfire and thought about his wife. He was sorry that he had been unkind and unpleasant. His heart was full of sorrow.

Then the Great Spirit, looking into the man's heart and seeing that he was sad, asked, "Would you like to have your wife back?"

The husband answered, "Oh, if she would return to me, I would never quarrel with her again!"

When the Great Spirit heard the man's promise, he decided to help him. So he started out to find the man's wife. At last, he saw her. She had been walking nearly all day,

and was now moving slowly with bowed head.

Quickly, the Great Spirit made a patch of beautiful blueberries spring up by the roadside. But the sorrowful woman did not even look at them.

Then the Great Spirit said to himself, "I will make some delicious red raspberries grow near her path. Surely she will like them!"

But the woman, with head still bowed, passed by, not heeding them.

Once more the Great Spirit tried to attract her attention. This time, he planted a tree filled with luscious, dark red cherries near the path. But once again the woman paid no attention. Then he planted wild fruits of many varieties along the road. Still she would not notice them.

Finally, the Great Spirit said to himself, "This time I must do my very best."

So he created a patch of strawberries, the first strawberries that had ever been made. When the woman saw them, she stopped at once and began to gather them eagerly.

While she was busy picking the beautiful red berries, the husband had time to catch up with her. He was very happy to find her. She gave him some of the sweet, red berries, and they ate and ate!

After they had eaten all they wanted, they returned home together. And they made a solemn vow that they would never quarrel again for they really loved each other.

The Chippewas called the strawberry "Odamin" which means "heart berry."

When the World Was Young

Nine

HOW THE EARTH WAS MADE

In the beginning, before the creation of the earth, the world was one large expanse of water. One day as the Great Spirit floated about with all the animals, he wished for a grain of sand that he might make some land so that men and animals could live on it. All that he needed was a grain of sand for this task.

"Let me dive to the bottom of this Great Water for some sand," suggested the beaver. "I feel sure that I can get some." The Great Spirit told this brave animal all about the dangers of such an undertaking, but the beaver still wished to try. Finally, the Great Spirit gave him permission.

Soon the beaver, promising to return speedily, started swimming toward the bottom. When the sun had set twice and morning had dawned again, and the beaver had not returned, the other animals became anxious. "Beaver must have drowned," they said sorrowfully. However, some time later, he came up breathless and completely exhausted. After he had rested, he told the Great Spirit that although he had narrowly escaped several sea monsters and had swum

continuously, yet he had been unable to reach the bottom.

Then the Great Spirit called upon the otter to try. This animal slipped noiselessly away and soon disappeared in the depths of the water. He stayed down even longer than the beaver. At last, when the otter arose to the surface, the other animals dragged him, almost senseless, to a shallow spot. When he was revived he said, sorrowfully, that he had not found any sand at the bottom of the great water.

After these two attempts, the Great Spirit and almost all the animals were ready to give up, but the little muskrat rose and said, "Let me try, O Great Spirit."

"You are very small. Do you think that you have the strength?"

"My heart will not fail."

"Go then," said the Great Spirit.

Immediately, the little muskrat dived and stayed down

all day and through the night. All during this time, the animals grieved and wailed, "He is dead. He must be dead."

And they were right, for the next morning they found the muskrat's body floating on the water. Picking it up, they noticed that all four of his little paws were shut tightly. When the animals forced three of the paws open, they found nothing within, but upon opening the last one, they discovered one grain of sand tightly clutched within it.

Then the animals knew that the muskrat had succeeded. He had reached the bottom of the Great Water. With that one grain of sand, the Great Spirit made the beautiful earth.

Ten

THE ORIGIN OF THE RACES

After the Great Spirit had made the earth, with beautiful trees, pretty flowers, broad rivers, and deep lakes, he rested and said, "My work is good and beautiful. Someone must live on this earth and be happy."

Turning to the Lesser Spirit on his right, who assisted him, he commanded, "Go make a man to live on and enjoy this beautiful earth!"

Eager to obey the Great Spirit's will, the Lesser Spirit immediately pushed off in his canoe and paddled to the region which is now called Minnesota. Now in this land, he found some white clay. Taking it, he molded it into a fine figure with broad shoulders, well-formed limbs, and a fine head. After he had covered the top of the head with brown moss, he breathed into this clay image the breath of life. Immediately, a tall, fair-complexioned figure arose and stood beside him. Then the Lesser Spirit took this beautiful figure back to the Great Spirit who looked upon the white face and cried, "No, not good!" Him white man!" Imme-

diately, the Great Spirit sent the white man across the ocean to Europe.

The Great Spirit still wanted a creature who could enjoy all the beauty of the universe. To satisfy this desire, he called another spirit to him. This one, the Great Spirit sent into the deep South in the vicinity of New Orleans. Here this Lesser Spirit found black muck. From it, he fashioned a huge, strong figure. He took some of the black and withered moss at the foot of the trees, changed it into hair, and covered the top of the figure's head with it. Then he breathed into this magnificent form the breath of life and carried the living creature back to the Great Spirit. Again the Great Spirit shook his head, sighed with disappointment, and said, "No, not good! Him black man. Send him to Africa."

In a few days, the Great Spirit travelled by canoe and journeyed through the forests until he reached the Rocky Mountains. From the brown soil, he made a figure with high cheek bones and a tall, sinewy form. When an eagle flew low and watched curiously, the Great Spirit plucked a feather from its wing and thrust it into the long, straight, black hair of the form he had molded. After the Great Spirit had breathed upon the eyes and lips of his creation, the figure arose. Then shading his eyes with his hand, the creature stood gazing upon the plains and the mountains. "Ugh!" said the pleased Great Spirit. "Him, good Indian! He can stay here."

Eleven

MACKINAC ISLAND

Long ago, a great Manitou called Manabozho was eager to find a place to live. He wanted the most beautiful spot in all the world for his home. In his search, he walked all over the country. At last, he thought, "I must get somewhere so that I can look at all the earth at one time. I cannot tell which spot is the loveliest when I view them one by one. I must go where I can see them all at the same time." Therefore, Manabozho climbed into the sky and then looked down upon the earth. As he gazed about, he saw Mackinac Island. He knew it was the place that he wanted! It looked like a huge green turtle. It humped out of the deep blue waters of the Straits of Mackinac. He made it his home at once. Then he invited the spirits of the earth, air, and water to come there to live with him. The Indians called these spirits the Giant Fairies.

The Chippewas believed that these spirits made a big rock bridge, called Arch Rock, so that the island would have a fine gateway. A long stairway leads to the top of this rock. People use the top of the rock for a bridge.

Sugar Loaf Rock is the home of the Great Manabozho.

59

The big hole at the base of Sugar Loaf Rock is called the Devil's Bake Oven.

Manabozho was never disappointed in his choice of a home. He knew that when the Great Spirit formed the land, he steadied the world by putting his hand gently on some fertile soil. When he raised it, the imprint of his whole hand could easily be seen. It was shaped like a mitten. The thumb of the mitten lies by Lake Huron and Saginaw Bay. The Indians, as you know, called this land Michigan which means Big Water.

Often the Indians from the mainland paddled their

canoes over to Mackinac Island. They brought Manabozho venison and warm furs. He in turn was good to the Indians. He kept the lakes and streams stocked with fish, and the forests filled with many animals. He did it so well that Michigan is still regarded as a vacation land.

Twelve

THE FORMATION OF THE
SOUTH FOX AND NORTH FOX ISLANDS

A long, long time ago, in the woods of Northern Michigan there was a great timber wolf. He was a very cruel wolf, for he often killed the smaller animals. Not one would he spare. The little animals were very much afraid of him. Some trembled and others hurried away whenever they saw him. Now Manabozho was the friend of the animals. He felt sorry for them. He did not wish them to be afraid and unhappy. He knew that the great timber wolf had killed many of his animal friends. At last, Manabozho thought that something must be done to stop the big, bad wolf. He decided he must get rid of him. Manabozho was not sure of the best plan. He thought and thought and thought! But Manabozho was very, very clever; and so, at last, he thought of a plan to outwit the wolf. Now Manabozho knew that the timber wolf loved a race. So he proposed that he and the timber wolf should run a race between North Port

Point and Harbor Springs. The wolf thought this would be great fun. The wolf was a fast runner, and he was sure that he could win. The wolf wanted to start at once, but Manabozho said that they must make some rules. They decided on two. One was that the race should begin just before dawn. The other was that the loser must leave the country forever.

Now Manabozho wanted very much to beat the great timber wolf. He knew that the small animals could never be safe and happy while their enemy was around.

At last, dawn came. The two got ready to start. The timber wolf started running along the shore of Lake Michigan. He liked to feel the soft sand and hear the lapping of the waves on the shore. He was happy as he hurried along the beach toward Harbor Springs. Now Manabozho knew that the wolf could run much faster than he. He decided that he could beat the wolf only by using his wits. Instead of running along the shore, Manabozho made another plan. He picked up large pieces of earth and clumps of trees. Then he threw them before him into Lake Michigan. He used them for steppingstones. He named some pieces of earth South Fox Island and other pieces North Fox Island. By jumping upon them, he was able to take a short cut

across the water. In this way, he reached Harbor Springs long before the wolf arrived there. All the small animals were very happy when Manabozho won. They were pleased that he had outwitted the great timber wolf. After the wolf left the country, the small animals lived safely and happily. Now this race was the reason that no great timber wolves live in Northern Michigan and why North and South Fox Islands lie in the lakes.

Thirteen

WHY BEES CAN STING

Long ago, bees were at the mercy of anything that chose to rob them, for they had no means of defending themselves or their possessions. No one could imagine how much trouble they had in keeping their honey from being stolen! All the animals and birds liked it, but the bears seemed to enjoy its sweetness most of all. They never seemed satisfied and were always ready for more of it. To discourage these plunderers, the bees hid their combs with their six-sided wax cells in hollow trees and in the clefts of high rocks. Yet the bears, with their sharp noses, were ever on the lookout to find these hiding places. Often the birds with long beaks sucked the fragrant honey out of the hollow tree trunks. Even the squirrels stole it.

The poor bees didn't know what to do! They searched for more flowers but they died in the fall, and so the bees couldn't gather any more nectar from them. Consequently, it often happened that whole swarms starved in the long winter because they had no honey. It was their only winter food. In fact, there was so little to eat that all these four-winged, hairy insects were in danger of being destroyed. At last, the bees stopped working together and divided into small groups. They stored just enough honey to keep them alive from season to season. Yet even under this plan, their hives were plundered.

In spite of their industry, the bees were constantly troubled. They were about ready to give up when they heard a report that Wakonda, the Strong Spirit, was planning on visiting his friends. This visitor announced that he was willing to help all who were having real troubles.

As soon as Wakonda arrived, the bees hurried to him. They carried with them a present of delicious honey which they had managed to hide from the bears. The Strong Spirit received the bees kindly. When he had eaten the honey, he said, "What can I do to help you?" Then the bees told him of their trouble.

Wakonda was angry and stamped his feet when he realized how mean the animals had been to these busy creatures. Then he remained quiet for a while as though he were trying to decide what would be the best way to take care of this problem. At length, he said, "I shall need several days to think about what would be the best thing to do. Come back in three days. By that time, I shall have a plan to help you." This promise pleased the bees. They told their relatives, the wasps and hornets, of Wakonda's promise.

Three days later the bees, accompanied by the hornets and wasps, returned to the meeting place. The Strong Spirit was surprised to see the bees' companions. He was not quite certain how to treat them for they did not have such a fine reputation for industry and thrift as the bees. Consequently, he asked them some pointed questions about their work. Since the bees, relying on the Strong Spirit's promise, were no longer so worried and distressed, they gave Wakonda favorable reports about their companions.

Then Wakonda turned to the bees and said, "I like you because you are industrious. You work in summer to prepare for winter. You are not like the lazy grasshopper that plays all day in the summer sunshine. Because you are workers, I shall give each of you a weapon that will keep the birds and animals away." Then he gave some stings to the wasps and hornets, too. Immediately all the bees and their companions thanked the Strong Spirit for this helpful gift.

Thereafter, because of Wakonda's generosity, the bees did not have to search for hiding places in which to store their honey. They often chose tall, hollow trees as storehouses. The big knotholes in the trunks served for doors. In these trees, the bees could make the honeycomb and fill it.

However, the bears were not easily discouraged and soon found these bee trees and began to climb them. They put their paws into the holes to get the sticky sweets. Immediately, the bees stung the bears on their noses, about their eyes, and on their lips. When the needlelike weapon pierced the skin, the bears howled with rage and fear. At first, they were puzzled and tried to fight the bees. When the rest of the bees heard the growling bears, they came in great numbers and joined in the fight. They stung the bears fiercely. At last, the bears, growling with rage and pain, were forced to run away and leave the honey.

Ever since, any other creature that troubles the bees is like to be badly stung, too.

Fourteen

THE FIRST BUTTERFLIES

When the Great Spirit planned to create the earth and mankind, he decided to make the land first. "I shall make a beautiful home for people," he said to himself. "I shall put mountains, lakes, rivers, plains, deserts, and forests upon the earth. It shall be such a beautiful place that all people will be happy there and live in peace."

Thereupon, the Great Spirit covered the earth with a carpet of green. He planted flowers of many varieties and colors to bloom in the fields. He made great forests and filled them with birds and animals. He formed the lakes and broad rivers teeming with many kinds of fish. Then he piled up great masses of solid rock that towered thousands of feet into the air. "My children will like the great rivers, the numerous lakes, the fertile fields, and the deep forests," said the Great Spirit, "for they are beautiful and useful. But how shall I get them to love the mountains? Even though I love them, they look cold and bare. How can I get my people to go to the mountains and learn to love them as I do?"

Over that question, the Great Spirit pondered deeply.

At last, he made many little shining stones. Some were red, some blue, some green, some yellow, and some shone with all the lovely tints of the rainbow. The Great Spirit then said, "I shall hide these stones in the cracks and crevices of the mountains. Men will come to find them, and in this way, they will learn to love the mountains."

As the Great Spirit looked at the stones which he had made, he realized that they were very beautiful. Among them were emeralds, turquoise, rubies, sapphires, diamonds, and opals. He said to these lovely stones, "I shall not hide all of you in the rocks of the mountains and in the earth. You must be out in the sunshine where men can admire you. I want the little children who cannot go to the mountains to see your beauty."

Just at that moment, the South Wind came by. He sang of the forests filled with oak, maple, spruce, and pine, and praised the graceful white birches and the silvery aspen. He chanted of the colorful song birds nesting in the leafy trees and of the meadows filled with flowers of every hue. He recalled the pleasures of summer days and summer evenings beside the clear blue water. All the beauty of day and night was in his song.

When the Great Spirit heard the South Wind's song, he said, "Dear South Wind, here are some beautiful things for you to take to your summer home. The little children will like their lovely colors and all men who love beauty will admire their loveliness." As soon as the Great Spirit stopped speaking, all the stones before him stirred with new life and lifted themselves lightly on their many-colored wings. They fluttered away in the glorious sunshine of that summer day like "winged flowers."

Thus it was that the first butterflies like the Black and Tiger Swallowtails, the Monarch, the Painted Beauty, and

the American Copper came from the beautiful thought of
the Great Spirit. In their wings were the colored stones
which he did not wish to hide away in the mountains.

Fifteen

WHY THE WEATHER IS CHANGEABLE

The aged chiefs of long, long ago liked to tell about two, lively Indian brothers, Nanabojo and Peepuckewis. Like most brothers, they did not always agree. These two young braves were always blamed by their elders for the dozen different kinds of weather that Michigan has in the region of the Great Lakes. This was the story which the aged chiefs told:

"Once Nanabojo and Peepuckewis ran a foot race from the far South to the Great Lakes. From the very start, Nanabojo was in the lead. All nature smiled as he ran swiftly along, because he himself was lighthearted and pleasant. The sun shone brightly, the birds sang, and little girls scattered gay flowers in his pathway. The squirrels, deer, bears, and all the other creatures of the wood played happily. They said, 'Here comes Nanabojo, our friend. He makes the pleasant weather.'

"All summer, as he moved northward, every day was warm and bright. There were no signs of frost, no thunder storms and no cyclones.

"Now it wasn't long before Peepuckewis became angry

72

at being left so far behind in the race. He stamped his feet. He forced himself to run faster and faster until he finally began to catch up with Nanabojo. He noticed, too, that wherever Nanabojo went the weather became really beautiful and that flowers bloomed and birds sang. As he raced along, Peepuckewis became more and more jealous every minute. He scowled, frowned, and growled as he hurried northward. His mind was filled with bitter thoughts. He decided to put a sudden stop to his brother's pleasant jour-

73

ney, to punish the earth, and to keep his smiling brother from winning the race.

"With this purpose in mind, Peepuckewis scooped up water in his hands. He threw it high into the air and commanded the winds to help him make some bad weather. First, he asked South Wind to blow a hot, dry breath that would bake the earth and dry up all the growing things. Next, he invited East Wind to bring rain to cause all the rivers to overflow and make floods. He made the clouds gather in front of the sun, so that Nanabojo would lose his way. But every time that Nanabojo looked back and smiled, away would go the clouds, and the sun would come out again, brighter than ever.

"Still Peepuckewis would not give up his plan. He called West Wind to come quickly with his frost, hail, and sleet. In a short time, the earth shivered because of the West Wind's icy breath.

"By autumn, Nanabojo had reached the Great Lakes. Because he needed to rest, he camped on the sandy shore of beautiful Lake Michigan. It was in the month of October. At this time, there was a spell of fair and warm weather and the leaves of the trees and shrubs were turning to red and gold. A lovely, smoky haze had settled down over the earth. Nanabojo rested in the peace of a lovely Indian summer.

"But Peepuckewis was not asleep, nor would he let his brother rest any longer. At this time, he ordered the fierce North Wind to bring the snow and cold. Of course, with this commotion, Nanabojo just had to wake up and hurry on. But every now and then, he would look back and smile, and his pleasant face never failed to bring the sunshine.

"By this time Peepuckewis was now very close; in fact, he was almost upon his brother's heels. He was growing

74

angrier and angrier every minute. In his fury, he ordered all the winds to blow and bluster at the same time. In the great confusion which followed, the two brothers turned and passed onward into the far West."

To this day, whenever the weather changes quickly and often, the aged Indians will say: "Nanabojo and Peepuckewis are near us. They are running their race."

Sixteen

THE ORIGIN OF MOSQUITOES

Long ago, when people dressed in deerskins, there lived an Indian chief, Souwanas, who was known for his industry. Often it was necessary for him to work in dirty places. At the end of the day, or whenever his work was finished, Souwanas always wished to put on clean clothes. Although he had several changes of clothing, he never seemed to have any clean ones when he needed them.

Now it was the duty of every squaw to scrape and clean her family's clothes and keep them in repair, but Waubeno, Souwanas' wife, was lazy and would not do the tasks that were required of her. She often neglected her work to gossip with the neighboring squaws. For a while, Souwanas was very patient with his wife. He knew she was strong and able, but that she was young and gay. At first, he felt sure that as she grew older she would learn to take her household tasks more seriously, and so he tried to overlook her shortcomings.

Many moons passed, yet Waubeno seemed to grow even more careless than she had been as a young wife. In fact, she didn't even keep herself tidy and neat. She often failed to cook food for her family. The truth is that Souwanas and the children were neglected most of the time.

One spring, the Indians received word that Wakonda, the Strong Spirit, was coming to visit them. He wished to see how the people were getting along. Although he was Souwanas' relative, he didn't often visit him and the Indians. Upon hearing of his proposed visit, all the Indians began making great preparations to please him, for this Strong Spirit could grant great favors, but if he were displeased, he would heap all kinds of injuries upon the Indians. As soon as Souwanas heard the news, he hurried home to tell Waubeno of the approaching visit of their relative.

Of course, Souwanas wished to be neatly dressed when Wakonda came; therefore, he asked his wife to have his clothes clean and the children washed and dressed. "Let's show Wakonda what a fine family we have," he urged. As the time drew near for the guest to arrive, the chief tried repeatedly to persuade Waubeno to clean the wigwam and to make herself tidy, but Waubeno always answered, "There is no hurry."

On the day that Wakonda was expected, Souwanas was very much disgusted when he found that he had no clean clothes. He was so very angry that he threatened to beat his wife. This punishment was the only way that Souwanas could get Waubeno to do her work, for she was afraid of a whipping. While Souwanas and his wife were quarreling bitterly, Wakonda suddenly appeared at the entrance to the wigwam. When Souwanas saw him, he told the Strong Spirit of the difficulty he was having with his irresponsible squaw and of her refusal to do her work.

Wakonda glanced around the wigwam. Everywhere he saw evidences of Waubeno's carelessness and idleness, for

the pots were not washed, the blankets hadn't been aired, and the floors were unswept. Then Wakonda, turning to the chief said, "A lazy, gossipy wife is a disgrace to her husband and an annoyance to all around her. Take some of the dirt that clings to your clothes and throw it at your wife." Souwanas obeyed Wakonda. Immediately the particles of dirt were changed into bloodthirsty mosquitoes which bit the indolent squaw.

Ever since, and especially on warm days of early summer when the mosquitoes come singing and stinging, we think of the lazy woman who must be blamed for these pests which have continued to irritate and annoy mankind.

New and Old Animal Friends

Seventeen

WHY THE CAT ALWAYS FALLS UPON HER FEET

"I'm too tired to walk farther in this forest until I get some rest," said Manabozho wearily. The sun was high overhead when Manabozho lay down on the ground at the foot of a tree. Soft, green moss grew all about him. The sun shone through the leaves and made spots of light and shadow on the ground. As he lay resting, he heard the songs of the birds, the buzz and the hum of insects, and the wind rustling the leaves of the trees. A feeling of peace and quietness stole over Manabozho. Soon all the music of the forest lulled him to sleep.

While Manabozho was fast asleep, a large, poisonous snake came gliding noiselessly through the grass. It lifted its head and saw Manabozho lying at the foot of the tree. "I will kill him!" it hissed. "I could have eaten that cat yesterday, if that man hadn't called out, 'Watch, little cat, watch!' Now it will be his turn to feel my fangs!"

Closer and closer crept the poisonous snake. Manabozho stirred in his sleep. He mumbled, "Watch, little cat, watch!"

81

At this warning, the snake withdrew a bit, but soon noticing that Manabozho's eyes were closed, it again went closer. It hissed loudly and made ready to strike. Manabozho did not move.

Upon a high branch of a tree directly above Manabozho's head lay a little cat. She had seen the snake when it came from the thicket, and had watched it glide through the grass

and come closer and closer to Manabozho. She heard it hiss. The little cat's body quivered with anger and shook with fear, for it was very little. She knew the snake was very powerful. "Manabozho has been very good to me," she thought. "I cannot let the snake bite him." In the next instant, she leaped down upon the ugly snake.

Oh, how angry the snake was! It hissed and its eyes looked like balls of fire as it struck wildly at the little cat. The brave cat leaped again and again upon the snake's head. At last, the snake lay dead beside the sleeping Manabozho.

When Manabozho awoke, the cat was lying near the dead snake. Manabozho realized at once that this cat had saved his life. He stroked it gently and said, "You brave creature! You saved my life. What can I do to show my gratitude, and to honor you for your brave fight?" Then Manabozho picked the cat up in his arms and sat quietly stroking it. At last he exclaimed, "I know what I shall do! You have sharp eyes and keen ears. You can run swiftly. Hereafter, you shall be known over all the earth as the friend of man and you shall always have a home in man's home. You jumped from the high tree to kill the poisonous snake. Now as long as you live, you shall be able to leap wherever you will and always fall upon your feet."

Eighteen

WHY THE RABBIT HAS LONG EARS

One day the owl, known as a very wise bird and the chief of all the animals, summoned them to meet on the lake shore on the following afternoon. The message said, "I have some very important things, for the good of all the animals, to discuss with you. I want all of you to be present." The animals began immediately to get ready to go.

The next day, the owl went to the meeting place. As soon as he arrived, he looked over the assemblage to see whether all of the animals were present.

"Where is the rabbit?" he asked. No one in the crowd had seen the rabbit nor could tell of his whereabouts.

"I must find him and bring him here," said the owl.

"Rabbit! Rabbit!" he shouted. Now the rabbit had hidden in a dense clump of bushes. He was sleepy and did not want to be disturbed.

"Rabbit! Rabbit!" called the owl again. Then he hooted loudly several times as a reminder of the meeting.

Now, of course, the rabbit had heard the owl the first time that he called, but he didn't want to go to the council and so continued to pretend that he did not hear. He lay down under the bushes, closed his eyes, and pretended to sleep.

After the owl had called twice or three times more, he became impatient and shouted, "Rabbit, if you do not obey and come to the council at once, your ears will grow. They will keep on growing until you answer and come."

The rabbit thought the owl's threat was a big joke. He laughed and said to himself, "How could that stupid, old owl make my ears grow? He would like to scare me because he can't find me. He certainly can't see very well during the day. He would find it very difficult to find me here in this clump of thick bushes."

And so the rabbit didn't answer.

But it wasn't very long before the rabbit's ears began to feel queer. "What can be the matter with my ears?" he cried as he put his right foot upon the top of his head. He felt his soft right ear carefully and then examined his left one in the same manner. "I do believe they are growing!"

he said with surprise and alarm. Then he waited a little while; he wondered what he had better do. He grew calmer as he lay on the cool ground. Again he laughed at his fears and said, "That solemn old owl with his large head and eyes, surrounded with feather disks, and his short beak can't frighten me!" But before long he again felt a queer itching sensation near his ears. He raised his foot again to his head. His ears had grown twice as long!

"Oh, I'd better answer!" exclaimed the terrified rabbit. Then he shouted as loudly as he could, "I hear, Owl. I am coming!" He immediately started for the council.

Now as soon as the rabbit answered, his ears stopped growing. But how the animals laughed when they saw the rabbit's long ears!

The rabbit was very much ashamed of his appearance. He humbly begged the owl to make his ears short again. But the wise old owl refused, and so the rabbit, because of his disobedience, has had long ears ever since.

Nineteen

WHY THE BEAR IS CLUMSY

Long, long ago when the Great Spirit created animals of all kinds to live upon the beautiful earth, he made plans for their happiness. "I want all my creatures to enjoy the green fields, the broad rivers, the deep woods, the fertile valleys and the good earth. I shall provide comfortable and suitable homes for each of them that peace and good will may prevail everywhere," he declared.

As soon as these homes were ready, the Great Spirit summoned the animals one by one to come to him. The ground hog came first. The Great Spirit said to him, "I want you to live in a hole on a beautiful hillside. When the cold winter comes, the snow will pile high in great drifts and will cover the doorway of your hole. You will be cozy and warm inside and there you can enjoy undisturbed sleep throughout the long winter."

"Nobody could ask for a finer home!" exclaimed the well-pleased ground hog. "Thank you, Great Spirit."

Soon the beaver appeared. Then the Great Spirit said, "I want you to dig a long tunnel at the bottom of the pond and make a lodge. Make the tunnel deep. Other animals must not be able to find the doorway to your home. Build the lodge of branches, sticks, and logs and fill in the cracks with grass and mud. The roof of your lodge should rise above the water. May you and your family be happy there."

"I am well pleased, for my home will be safe and strong," said the busy beaver. "My fur will keep me warm, too. Thank you, kind Spirit."

The Great Spirit in turn talked to each of the animals. Some of them he sent to the regions where the days are always warm. Fur-covered animals went where the air is thin and cold. For the monkey and his family, the Great Spirit chose the thick jungles with hanging vines where all of them could climb the trees, jump from one to another, and swing on the branches by their tails. The birds found their homes in countries where there were beautiful trees, tall grass, and bright flowers. Often the flowers were the same color as birds' beautiful plumage. The Great Spirit provided food for all his creatures and the kinds that they liked the best.

"Now that all have shelter and food," the Great Spirit said to himself, "I must make them safe from their enemies. They must have the gait and habits which they need. I must make the deer able to run so swiftly that none can catch it for men will want to kill this beautiful creature for food. The rabbit with its soft fur can be safe from its enemies by hopping quickly and lightly over the ground."

"The turtle will not have to run fast, for I shall cover its back with a thick, hard shell. When something raps its shell sharply, in will go the turtle's head, legs, and even its tail. Nothing can hurt it, I feel sure," said the Great Spirit.

Soon the donkey with its big, flappy ears, stood before the Great Spirit and brayed loudly. "You may walk slowly,

too," said his maker. "But I shall give you sharp heels that you may kick anything that troubles you."

Now all the animals except one liked the Great Spirit's gifts and thanked him for them. That animal was the bear. At first, he merely sulked and growled. Then he said gruffly, "I want to run as fast as the deer."

Now the bear really did not need to run fast. The Great Spirit had created him with sharp claws, strong paws, and long teeth. Besides, because men did not care to eat his tough and coarse flesh, he had no real reason to run from them. But even though the bear had his strong features pointed out to him, he was still displeased and said, "I want to run down the hill very fast."

The Great Spirit shook his head.

Then the bear became terribly angry. He went around muttering and growling. He picked quarrels with all the other animals and was most unpleasant.

At last, the Great Spirit lost his patience. He decided to punish the ugly creature. "Such behavior has gone far enough!" said the Great Spirit sharply. "Hereafter, you shall be the most awkward of all the beasts. You must shuffle from one side to another on the trail. When you try to run fast, you will tumble. You are so mean and unpleasant that no animal wants you around. Go at once and live far away in the woods. There you will not trouble anyone when you are cross."

The bear walked away clumsily. He had to obey the Great Spirit's command, but he growled as he did it.

Twenty

WHY THE RACCOON HAS RINGS ON ITS TAIL

Many moons ago, two old Indian brothers named Souwanas and Sagastao lived together in a wigwam. Some young braves built them a wigwam in a safe, quiet spot near a lake. Others made pots and dishes for their cooking and kept a large pile of wood cut for their use. That these poor, blind men might get water from the lake without danger, another thoughtful Indian fastened a rope to guide Souwanas and Sagastao from the wigwam to a post on the edge of the lake. Often friendly squaws brought food to these unfortunate men. The other Indians in the region did whatever they could to make these poor, blind men comfortable.

Now although both Souwanas and Sagastao were often lonely and felt discouraged because of their blindness, yet they lived happily together. They divided their work equally. On the day that Souwanas did the cooking, Sagastao carried the water and brought the wood for the fire. On the next day, each did the work which the other had done on the previous one. Often they found it necessary to rest after their labors for the weaknesses of old age had come upon them.

Late one afternoon, after Souwanas had worked hard, he lay down to rest. When he awoke, he said to Sagastao, "My brother, I feel hungry; let us have our supper now."

"I'd like it, too," answered Sagastao. "I feel sure that the meat must be cooked. You get some fresh water while I finish getting the meal."

Now it happened on this late afternoon in the fall, while a raccoon was prowling around in the twilight looking for food, he found the end of a rope which was tied to a post. He was puzzled and wondered where it led. He followed it to the blind men's wigwam. When he reached there, he raised the flap of skins before the door and peeked in. There he saw the two, old brothers sleeping near the fire. The raccoon could smell something cooking which he thought

must be very good. "I'll wait around and try to get some of that meat for my supper," he said to himself.

Later he crept noiselessly into the wigwam without Sagastao's knowing it. Then he eagerly watched him finish preparing the meal. Soon it was ready. The supper consisted of eight pieces of a bear's brain, which the aged man put in a wooden bowl.

By this time, Souwanas had returned with a bucket of water. The brothers sat down to their meal. Each took a piece of meat from the bowl. While they ate, they talked about the last visit they had had with some of their Indian friends.

During their conversation, the raccoon stealthily seized four pieces of the meat from the bowl, took them outside and ate them greedily. A little later, Sagastao reached into the bowl to get another piece of meat. When he discovered that only two pieces were left, he said in his surprise, "You must have been hungry, Souwanas, to have eaten so fast. I have eaten only one piece of meat. There were eight pieces in the bowl; now there are only two left."

"I did not eat them, Sagastao," answered Souwanas. "I've had only one."

"You must have," insisted his brother. "You know that I can't see so you probably ate them. You are often greedy when you are hungry."

Sagastao's remark made Souwanas angry. The blind men continued arguing and saying unkind things to each other. The raccoon, that had returned to the wigwam for more food, seemed to enjoy the trouble he had made, and presently he struck each blind man a sharp blow on his face. Not realizing who had struck them, the blind men began fighting fiercely. Soon they had upset the bowl containing the rest of their supper.

While the old men were quarreling and fighting, the raccoon quickly snatched the bowl and the rest of the meat. Then, shouting with laughter, he rushed out of the wigwam. As soon as Souwanas and Sagastao heard the shrill laughter, they realized that someone had played a mean trick on them. They stopped fighting and apologized to each other.

In the meantime, the raccoon still pleased with his cleverness was awkwardly carrying the wooden bowl in which lay the two remaining pieces of the bear's brains. As he sauntered along, he continued to laugh loudly. Presently, he met Manabozho, who said, "Good evening, Raccoon. I heard you laughing. Why are you so very happy?"

Now the raccoon didn't know that the person addressing him was the Great Spirit, Manabozho. Boastingly, he told Manabozho how he had obtained the food and the bowl. As Manabozho listened to the raccoon's story, he became very angry.

At length he said, "I am Manabozho. Those poor, blind men are my brothers. You are a mean, selfish creature! For that mean trick, I'll teach you a lesson that you and your family will never have a chance to forget." Then he seized the raccoon and killed it. He carried it back to the blind men's wigwam and made a feast for them. Later Manabozho declared, "In the future, all raccoons must wear as many stripes on their tails as the number of pieces of meat that their relative stole from the poor, blind men."

Ever since that day raccoons have had ringed tails.

Twenty-one

HOW THE FOX WAS OUTWITTED

One day, a hungry fox decided to try to catch some doves that lived near him. He knew that they would make him a delicious dinner. He was puzzled as to how he could catch them. He felt sure that he would have to trap them by one of his sly tricks. While thinking about which one would be the best, he heard a woodpecker nearby.

The beautiful, red-headed bird was sitting on the side of a dead tree trunk, pecking and rapping hard, and singing a song.

"Good morning, Woodpecker," called the fox. "You seem happy and gay today."

"Oh, yes, indeed!" replied the woodpecker, resting on his stiff tail feathers. "I am very happy, but you look sad. What is troubling you?"

"I am sad," said the fox. "I am very fond of my neighbors, the doves, but they don't seem to like me and won't have anything to do with me. I tried to call on them, but they wouldn't let me in. I would like to get close to them."

"Well, that is too bad," said the woodpecker. Then he began pecking again and sang some more.

The fox continued to sit at the foot of the tree trunk while the woodpecker made a hole in it. "Perhaps, Woodpecker, if you would teach me your song so that I could sing it, the doves might let me in," suggested the fox.

"All right!" said the woodpecker, "I'll be happy to teach it to you." Then the woodpecker sang his song over and over until the fox could sing it too.

As soon as the fox was sure he knew the woodpecker's song, he hurried away to see the doves. When the fox arrived, some of the doves were out in the tall grass eating seed, and others were feasting on kernels of corn. When the doves heard the fox's big voice singing so queerly, they flew up suddenly with a whirr. Now the fox was so frightened and startled by the noise that he completely forgot his song. He couldn't think of a single word of it. He raced back to the woodpecker as fast as he could go to learn the song over again.

Now the woodpecker had been shocked by the fox's bad manners, for the latter had trotted off singing the song without even bothering to say "Thanks" for the help that he had received.

The beautiful bird said to himself, "If the fox ever comes back and bothers me again, I shall teach him a lesson." And so that he might be ready in case the fox returned, the woodpecker had found a short, thick stick. He burned the end of it in a fire until it glowed a bright red. Then he flew up and stuck the other end into the hole which he had previously pecked in the tree trunk.

By this time, the fox had come back to learn the song over again. He stood at the foot of the tree and called and called,

"I have forgotten your song, Woodpecker; you will have to sing it for me again."

But the woodpecker didn't answer.

Then the fox called a little louder. "I have forgotten your

song. You must teach it to me again. I want to learn it now."

Still there was no answer.

By this time, the fox was growing more angry every minute. He showed his sharp, white teeth. Finally he shouted, "If you do not sing to me, Woodpecker, I will eat you up."

There was no answer. The fox jumped as high as he could and snapped at the burning stick with his sharp teeth. Before he could drop it, the stick had scorched his nose so much that he wears a black nose to this very day.

Twenty-two

HOW BEAVER FOOLED THE PORCUPINES

"Did you steal my food?" anxiously inquired Beaver.

"No," answered Porcupine with a smile.

Beaver had worked hard all summer and fall to build a lodge. He had found a place along the stream where the bank was not steep. The bank was covered with poplars, birches, wild cherries, and willows. The bark, twigs, and leaves of these trees provided most of Beaver's food. The branches and twigs furnished the material for the dam and the lodge. In fact, no animal had been more busy than Beaver getting ready for winter. Porcupine made no such preparation. In winter, regardless of the weather, he often lived in one tree for weeks. He slept in the crotches and lived on the bark. Trees seemed to be all the dining room and bedroom that Porcupine needed for cozy winter living.

Beaver continued to glare at Porcupine.

"It is foolish for you to think that I could steal your food. One cannot steal food from supernatural beings. Both of us possess supernatural power," continued Porcupine.

Beaver realized that Porcupine was bluffing and was in no way deceived by his clever speech.

"You stole my food! I know you did!" said Beaver angrily. He tried to seize Porcupine with his teeth. But Porcupine's sharp spines and quills hindered his doing it. Porcupine resembled a cactus and had the same means for protection that a cactus has. But he was a climbing, gnawing, walking animal cactus. He stood facing Beaver for he was safest from his enemies when he stood still, with his spines sticking out in all directions. For a time, Beaver fought him fiercely, but, at last, poor Beaver was forced to give up. Porcupine had clawed and struck him with big coarse spines and small

ones, as thin as a needle. These barbs had worked steadily deeper into Beaver's face and body. Beaver's face was full of them when he reached his home.

Beaver's friends and relatives were terribly sorry for him. They pulled out the spines that clung like fish hooks in his body and nose. His father was so angry because of his son's ill-treatment that he called together all the Beaver People. He told them of his son's injury and bade them do something to punish the wrongdoer and to uphold the honor of their family. The Beaver People hurried to Porcupine's quarters. When they called to him, Porcupine thinking he was safe in the top of the tree was saucy and insulting to them. The Beaver People became very indignant. In a very short time, with their crunching chisel teeth, they gnawed down the tree where Porcupine had lodged. They seized Porcupine and carried him, in spite of his threats and objections, to a barren island. They left him there to starve.

Porcupine soon felt that he had not long to live. He had no food, for nothing grew on this island except two trees which could not be used for food. Porcupine called loudly to his friends, "Come help me or I shall starve." But he received no answer. Then he called to all his relatives. By this time, Porcupine was so weak from hunger that his relatives didn't hear his cries.

When Porcupine had given up all hope, he fancied he heard something whisper to him. It seemed to say, "Call upon Cold Weather. Call upon North Wind." At first, Porcupine didn't pay any attention to the voice. He thought that he had only imagined hearing it. Again the voice whispered, "Sing songs to the North Wind and you will be saved."

Porcupine was desperate and ready to try almost anything. He soon started to sing as loudly as he could:

> *"Come, North Wind, with your icy breath,*
> *Bring storms, snow, and freezing flakes;*
> *Let Cold Weather cover the lakes*
> *With a mantle of ice to save me from death."*

After a while the weather became very cold, a strong wind blew from the north, and the water became smooth with a layer of ice.

When the ice had become sufficiently thick to bear their weight, the Porcupine People, who had begun a wide search for their relative, crossed to the island to look for Porcupine. They rejoiced when they found him. He was so weak he could hardly walk and had to be carried to his home.

When Porcupine's family asked why Beaver had treated him cruelly, Porcupine told them that he had done nothing except eat Beaver's food. The Porcupines were angry that the Beavers had punished their relative unjustly. They thought that taking some food was a very small offense. Therefore they declared war on the Beavers. The two families fought for some time. Finally, the Porcupine Family was defeated. They still had a grudge against Beaver and so plotted to take his life.

At last, they managed to capture Beaver. They carried him to the top of a tall tree.

Because Beaver could not climb, they thought he would be in the same condition as Porcupine had been on the island. They wanted to give him a taste of his own medicine. How they smiled when they had placed him on the highest bough! They went home pleased with themselves. However, the pleasure over their clever deed didn't last long. They felt very foolish when they discovered that Beaver had eaten the tree downward from the top and had soon returned to his home.

Twenty-three

WHY THE TURTLE IS COVERED WITH SHELLS

"I'm tired and hungry. I need something to eat," said Manabozho, the Indian trickster, to himself as he started walking toward the village. As he approached it, he saw a little papoose with beady, black eyes, and coal black hair in front of a wigwam. The child was lying on its back with its big toe in its mouth. Manabozho laughed and laughed. He never before had seen a baby suck its toe. He stood fascinated by the papoose's agility.

Manabozho thought, "That was a clever trick. I can do anything that any other person can do. I'm going to try it myself." He sat down near the papoose, and took off his own left moccasin. Then he tried to put his big toe in his mouth, but he soon found that his knees and legs were stiff. He tried and tried, and in his effort fell over backward and hit his head. He rubbed the sore spot for a while and then it felt better. Manabozho was not easily discouraged and soon he was ready to try again. This time, he took off his other moccasin and attempted to put the big toe on his right foot into his mouth. He had no better luck. In fact, Manabozho was so fat and clumsy that he fell over on the ground. He could hardly get up.

The little papoose watched Manabozho's strange antics, and evidently thought them very funny for he laughed and laughed at the clumsy man. When Manabozho saw the child was laughing at him, he became angry and left at once. He was in a bad humor because he was hungry and his pride was hurt. He couldn't bear the thought that a small child had done something that he was unable to do. As he limped along stiffly, he came to a lake. On the shore,

some Indians were cooking some fish. When Manabozho told them that he was hungry, they gave him some food. He sat down on a log near the edge of the lake to eat the fish.

While he was eating, he thought of the papoose's feat. He decided to try once more. This time in his efforts to get his big toe into his mouth, he fell over backward and landed in the water with a loud splash. Now it happened that a mud turtle was lying just where Manabozho fell. Manabozho painfully pulled himself out of the mud and the mud turtle crawled out too. The mud turtle was startled and very much frightened.

He said sharply to Manabozho, "What do you mean by

jumping upon me? Don't you see that you have spoiled my shape? Now I shall be laughed at by all my race. Hereafter, look where you jump."

Manabozho felt sorry that he had hurt the poor turtle, for he loved the animals. He was ashamed, too, of his own awkwardness and determined to do something to help the poor creature that he had injured. Manabozho picked up two large shells from the shore; then he placed one shell over the turtle's back and the other one on the underside of its body. Manabozho felt sure that these hard shells would protect the injured animal so that it would never again have such a mishap. For whenever danger threatened, the turtle could pull its head and its legs between the shells. Ever since the accident, the turtle has continued to wear these hard shells around its body and has had no further trouble.

Strong Magic

Twenty-four

THE INDIAN SANDMAN

Weeng, the Indian Sandman, had many helpers. They were named little Weengs. These fairylike helpers were so tiny that no one could see them. In fact, it is believed that they were no bigger than specks. Besides, these tiny creatures were so nimble and quick that people couldn't keep track of them. They would light upon the forehead, and then hit a person on the head. The hard blow usually made him sleepy at once, but if the first blow was not enough, others were given until the drowsy person closed his eyes and fell into sound sleep.

It was the duty of the tiny Weengs to make any person whom they met sleepy. Some Weengs hid around babies' cradle boards; others perched nearby where someone was resting on a bearskin and still others liked to hide near a big fire where the older Indians were likely to sit. Then the Weengs brushed their wings over the eyes of the aged person who was resting and soon he sank into deep sleep.

Often, when a hunter went into the woods, the Weengs hid in his tobacco pouch. When he sat down to smoke, these tiny fairies flew out and threw their sleepy powder into his face. Then the hunter fell asleep. During this time, a deer or any other animals could pass by him unharmed. Often the hunter would have to return to his wigwam without getting any game. The Weengs played other tricks. Sometimes they made the Indian chief fall asleep in his canoe. Then it drifted too near the rapids and was upset. At other times, when a brave was standing guard, the Weengs made him fall asleep. They often bothered a war party near an enemy's country. They laughed when they made a squaw fall asleep while she was making bread and it burned up in the outdoor oven. The Weengs, at times, were real mischief makers!

However, they did many good things. They helped Indian children get the sleep they needed for health; they gave strength to persons whose bodies were tired, and they put worried people to sleep and made them forget their troubles.

The Indians wished to see how the Sandman looked, for they had never seen him. An Indian, named Iagoo, often bragged that he had seen Weeng. Iagoo claimed that one day, when he went hunting, somehow his dogs, that he loved, strayed away. They were such faithful companions that Iagoo got worried about them when half a day had passed and they had not returned. He called and called, but the dogs didn't come. Iagoo started searching for them at once. He walked through the woods for a long distance and encircled the forest several times. He took one trail after another and kept calling, but the dogs did not come running to him. He continued searching, for the dogs were his faithful friends.

Finally, he came to a spot where he found them in a deep sleep. Iagoo soon realized that they must have run very near to Weeng's house, and that he had put them to sleep. Iagoo

110

had a lot of trouble trying to get the dogs awake but, at last, they opened their eyes and recognized him. When Iagoo was ready to start home, he looked around and saw Weeng sitting on the branch of a tree just above the spot where the dogs had slept. Iagoo declared that the Sandman looked like a giant insect with many wings on his back, and that these wings made a low, deep, murmuring sound like falling water or waves gently lapping upon the shore.

Twenty-five

HOW THE SNAKE GOT ITS RATTLES

Often Manabozho, disguised as a hunter, walked into the forest. One day as he was walking by a wigwam on the edge of the woods, he heard a woman moaning and crying, "Oh, my child! Oh, my little papoose!" He knew something dreadful must have happened. Manabozho was a kind spirit; he loved the Indians and wished to help anyone who was in trouble. Therefore, he ran toward the wigwam, and found a young squaw with a very sick baby in her arms. When Manabozho tried to comfort the anxious mother, she told him that a big snake had crawled into her home, and had bitten her child who was lying asleep on the floor.

As soon as Manabozho heard the frantic squaw's story, he hurried into the woods. Soon he found a plant with a white flower. He spoke to it and said, "Henceforth, your roots shall be a remedy for snake bite." Then he took the roots of this plant back to the wigwam and showed the squaw how to pound the roots and make a drink to cure her sick baby. The mother obeyed Manabozho's orders. Soon she put a poultice on the papoose's leg and gave her a drink of the medicine. After a few days of careful nursing, the little papoose was well again.

The Indians were grateful to Manabozho for the gift of this plant which was thereafter known as snakeroot.

As soon as Manabozho was sure that this lovely little girl was recovering, he continued his journey. While walking along, he said to himself, "Now I must fix that snake so that he will not be able to do so much harm." In a short time, Manabozho came upon the cruel snake, sunning itself on the edge of a marsh. Manabozho scolded it for its meanness. He said, "You snakes, like other things, have the right to live. You have been given your place in the world and your work to do. Your work is to destroy mice, rats, frogs, toads, and other things that might become too numerous. You have poisons to defend yourself when you are attacked. You have no right to hurt anything which is not injuring you. It was only meanness that made you bite the little papoose when she was fast asleep. I'll fix you so that hereafter you cannot crawl quietly about and bite people."

Then Manabozho took a piece of wampum from one of the strings which he wore around his neck. He carved it into hard shells like large beads, and fastened them firmly

Strong Magic

to the snake's tail. Then, turning to the snake, he said, "From this day, all snakes like you shall have noisy rattles upon them. People will call you "rattle snakes." With these rattles, you will no longer be able to move without making a noise. Hereafter, people will be able to hear the rattles and get ready to fight you or to get out of your way before you can bite them."

Twenty-six

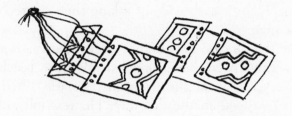

GLOOSKAP'S GIFTS TO THE THREE SEEKERS

Three young braves were very unhappy. They were dissatisfied with themselves and their manner of living. "Let us seek Glooskap," said Washoshee, at last. "He will help us!" Both Meyotao and Songitehe agreed that Washoshee's idea was a good one, and so the three Indian braves left home in the spring as soon as the birds returned from the South. All summer they journeyed over rivers, up mountains and through deep forests. Autumn came, and winter, and spring again; yet they had not found Glooskap. Still they would not turn back to their wigwams.

One day in midsummer, they came to a path and followed it until they reached a river that widened into a lake. The path encircled the lake and in places it was marked by blazed trees.

"There is a wigwam ahead!" cried Meyotao. "See the trees are blazed on the side toward us." They hurried on and came to a piece of land that stretched out into the lake. After they had climbed a hill, they saw a cloud of smoke rising at the end of the land. They hastened on and presently came to a wigwam.

When they entered, they saw a chief sitting near the

115

fire, smoking a pipe, and an aged squaw stirring a pot on the fire. A bearskin lay at the left of the door as though someone sat there.

"Welcome," said the chief. Then he made a place for the strangers to sit and, without asking their names, offered them his pipe.

While the braves sat resting, they heard a sound as though a canoe were being dragged upon the beach. Presently, the skin flap of the wigwam door was lifted and a young brave stood in the doorway. He was tall and thin. His clothes fitted neatly over his slender frame.

"Grandmother," he called, "here is some meat for you."

The old woman tottered to the door and picked up four beavers.

Immediately, she brought her skinning knife and began to prepare the meat for the pot. But her eyes were weak, and her hands trembled and soon she dropped the knife.

Then the chief spoke to the young brave and said, "Young brother, you cut up the meat!"

Muto, the young brave, obeyed the command. Then the aged squaw put the pieces of meat into the pot. When the meat had cooked, the family and the guests ate supper. The tails of the beavers, which the Indians regard as a delicacy, were given to the three braves, for Indians always give the best to their guests.

The travellers rested many days in the wigwam. During this time, the chief asked them no questions, but gave them the best food to eat and the softest blankets on which to sleep.

The old squaw seemed to grow more aged every day. Her hands shook so that she could hardly stir the fire when it was low. Her back became even more bent and painful than it had been when the travellers first saw her.

The guests pitied her. "Before long she will die," they thought.

One morning, as she was bending over the fire, the chief, turning to Muto, said, "Bathe your grandmother's face with water."

The young brave brought a bowl, filled it, and gave it to her that she might wash. As the water touched the old squaw's face, a change came over her. Her snow-white hair became black and glossy and her cheeks grew plump and rosy. Her bent back became straight as an arrow.

Soon she drew from a bag a garment of softest skin. She put it on. Then she stood before them, a woman, young, graceful, and beautiful. The travellers had never seen a lovelier woman.

"That man must be a magician!" whispered Washoshee to his companions. All of them were astonished and awed.

Then the chief turned to them and said, "Who are you? What is your mission?"

"We are braves searching for Glooskap, whom we wish to see."

"I am he!" said the chief. His face lighted up as he spoke. The travellers then saw that he was really Glooskap.

Then Songitehe said, "I am a wicked brave. I lose my temper quickly and speak ill of others. I wish to be good that men may love me. I need your help."

"I am poor," said Meyotao. "I am not able to kill enough deer and other game to keep my children from being hungry. I want to be rich that I may care for them and for others who need me."

When Washoshee spoke, he said, "I am ugly, and my back is crooked. I wish to be handsome so that all will welcome me into their wigwams. I want to have friends and be friendly."

Glooskap sat and smoked for a while. "You shall have what you have asked for," he said at last.

Then Glooskap took three boxes from his medicine bag. He gave one to each of the travellers. "When you reach your own village, you may open the boxes, but do not look inside of them until you arrive." Later, he gave the travellers suits of clothing made of beautiful, soft skins. "Put them on," he commanded.

When the three braves had thrown away their own worn-out garments and donned their new clothes, they were ready to depart.

"Which way do you journey to reach your village?" asked Glooskap.

"We do not know," replied Songitehe. "We were so many months coming here that we have lost our way. We do not know which way to go."

"I will guide you home," said Glooskap.

The next morning, Glooskap, after donning his head-dress and belt, led the travellers forth. By the time the sun was overhead, they had reached the top of a mountain. Then Glooskap, pointing to another peak in the distance, said, "That is near your home."

By mid-afternoon, the travellers had reached the top of the other mountain. The braves could not understand how they had reached it so soon.

Raising his arm and pointing with his finger, Glooskap said, "There is your village!"

Then the travellers looked and saw that they were in their own land.

Then Glooskap, after shaking hands with each one, left. With joyful hearts, the three braves climbed down the mountain and hurried home. They reached their village before sunset.

No one knew them when they arrived at their wigwams. "Where did you get such beautiful clothes?" inquired their friends in astonishment.

Then the braves told the story of what had happened during their absence. When they had finished, the braves opened their boxes. Within was a perfumed ointment which they rubbed over their flesh. Immediately, they were changed.

Washoshee, who had been ugly and hunchbacked, became so straight and handsome that he was welcomed into every wigwam.

Meyotao, the poor Indian, became a rich brave. He soon had an abundance of moose and deer, and fish fairly swarmed into his nets. He did not forget that he had been poor, but gave gladly to all who were in need.

Songitehe, who had been wicked and unkind, became gentle and good. Of all the gifts, his was the greatest one.

Twenty-seven

THE HUGE FOOD TREE

Long, long ago, Gitche Manitou, the Great Spirit of the Chippewa Indians, made a huge tree that bore all kinds of delicious fruits and vegetables. Rosy red apples, yellow pears, juicy peaches, mealy white potatoes, ears of tender corn, bunches of green bananas, red beets, and orange-colored carrots with feathery green foliage hung from its branches. All the Chippewas depended upon this gigantic tree for their food.

By-and-by, Gitche Manitou who looked down from the sky upon all the Indians became jealous of this huge tree which towered into the sky. At last, he commanded that it be cut down. A brave from each of the Indian families was given the task of carrying out the Sky Spirit's order. Soon the braves with saws, axes, and mallets began their work. Although these Indians worked hard, it took them a year and a day to cut down the tree because its bark was very thick and tough. At the end of that time, the tree fell to the ground with a crash like a great clap of thunder.

All the Indians were sorrowful over the loss of this giant tree. They loved it very much. Except for fish and game,

they had depended on it for their food supply. After the
loss of the tree they did not have sufficient food and often
suffered because of hunger. In their distress, the Chippewas
implored the Great Spirit for help.

After a while, Gitche Manitou was moved by the sorrow
of the Indians and said,

> "Good in this tree the Sky Spirit perceives
> Plant the branches and plant the leaves."

Once again the braves with the help of the squaws did as they were commanded, for the Indians always obeyed the Great Spirit. Wherever they put a branch or some leaves into the ground, soon a pear or apple tree, a potato vine, or one of the other fruits and vegetables sprang up. Thereafter, all the various foods that the giant tree had produced grew as separate plants, vegetables, and fruits, and had to be cultivated by the Indians.

Twenty-eight

THE DEVIL'S POND

The Devil's Pond was the name of a supposedly bottom-less pool of water, located near beautiful Harbor Point and Little Traverse. The Chippewas believed it was the home of the evil spirit, Mitchi-Manitou. They were terribly afraid of this evil spirit. Toward evening when the shadows of the sand dunes and of the pine trees could be seen on the surface of Devil's Pond, no Indian would go near it. For at that time, Mitchi-Manitou was accustomed to leave his watery home. Wandering about, he would cast an evil spell on anyone who had the misfortune to meet him.

It is said that long ago Mitchi-Manitou fell in love at first sight with Onaway. She was the beautiful daughter of a chief who lived on Mackinac Island. This lovely girl with gentle manners, glossy black hair, and a slender figure had many admirers. When the chief found out that Mitchi-Manitou was in love with Onaway, he was terribly distressed and worried. He rarely left the wigwam. He guarded Onaway carefully.

124

However, for the sake of food, he sometimes found it necessary to take his bow and arrow to hunt for the deer in the forest. When the need arose, he followed the shores of the island with his five-tined Indian spear for silver white-fish, Mackinaw trout, or sturgeon.

Whenever the chief left the wigwam, he took many precautions lest Onaway be kidnapped. He placed the lovely

125

girl on a bed of soft furs and skins in a birch-bark canoe, and set the small craft adrift among the tall reeds on the lee side of the island. Then he fastened it securely to the shore with a long basswood rope tied to a cedar tree.

Before setting out, the chief placed sacks of pemmican in the canoe. This was a very nourishing food. It was made of dried venison, crushed maize, and maple sugar. This mixture was pounded to a paste and mixed with suet and dried fruits. The chief knew that this food would satisfy Onaway's hunger during his absence. He went away contented, for he felt sure he had hidden his daughter where Mitchi-Manitou could never find her.

Probably because Mitchi-Manitou was an evil spirit and had unusual powers, he always knew or surmised the times when the chief left the wigwam. Immediately, he would start searching for the beautiful Onaway. He looked for many hours and searched every part of the island. At last, his search was successful. He immediately carried the lovely girl away to his home in Devil's Pond.

The chief returned from the hunt just in time to see his daughter being abducted. He pursued the kidnapper across the lake with all possible speed. He reached the pond just in time to see Onaway's beautiful dark braids floating on the surface of the pool as Mitchi-Manitou with the girl in his arms slipped back into his watery home.

The distracted father shouted and cursed Mitchi-Manitou. He vowed he would get revenge. The kidnapper only laughed with glee at the threats. Then the chief tried to bribe Mitchi-Manitou with promises of rich gifts, but the evil spirit was unmoved. At last, he shouted to the sorrowful father, "These are my only terms. You may reclaim your daughter when you have filled up the pool with sand."

Between Devil's Pond and Lake Michigan stand a num-

126

ber of sand dunes. They were made by the shifting sands of the lake shore. Sometimes the strong West Wind drove the sand over the dunes into Devil's Pond. Then the Chippewas used to say that the old chief was throwing handfuls of sand into the pond that he might reclaim his daughter.

After a while the white man arrived. During the lumbering days, he built a sawmill near Devil's Pond. Soon he dumped the sawdust into the bottomless pool. By this means, the pool was filled up much more quickly than it would have been otherwise.

Whether the old chief recovered his daughter or whether she chose to stay with Mitchi-Manitou in some other watery dwelling, no one seems to know.

Facing Danger

Twenty-nine

THE ORIGIN OF THE BOW AND ARROW

Often, while walking through the woods or in the middle of night as he lay on a bearskin, Osseo thought of his approaching sixteenth birthday. His heart was filled with joy and fear. In two moons, he would have to prove his courage by going hunting and bringing back in seven days something powerful and valuable. According to the tribal tradition, only thus could he show that he was worthy of the other braves' respect. Like most other young braves, Osseo wanted most of all to show what he could do and to be respected and honored by the tribe.

Osseo and his father had often talked about this test. Although the young brave was trustworthy and ambitious, his father feared, because his son was weak and small, that he would fail. However, no father in the tribe would openly doubt his son's ability, for to be doubted was a terrible disgrace. Consequently, in spite of his fears, the father spoke encouragingly, and offered prayers for Osseo when the young brave left on this important mission.

Osseo hurried to a part of the country where few Indians had ever been. Here he found many moose. These animals

131

were larger and stronger than any others he had ever seen. He was eager to kill one. Almost as soon as Osseo sighted the moose, he began throwing stones at them, but in spite of his efforts, he couldn't kill a single one. Then Osseo realized that because he lacked strength he would have to get very close to the animals to kill them, but to do so seemed impossible. Although he tried hard, at the end of the first day Osseo's efforts had been fruitless. Two days went by, then the third and fourth, and yet he hadn't killed a single one of the herd. He tried over and over again, but he couldn't hurl the rocks hard enough to wound the big animals. In fact, after he had thrown a few stones, he would have to rest before he had strength to try again. In the meantime, the moose would wander to a new feeding ground.

Although Osseo had prayed daily to the great goddess of nature to help him, nothing had happened during those four days. He had not suddenly become strong because of Arrometus' magic power, nor had a big moose suddenly fallen dead because of Osseo's powerful blow. The brave felt sad, discouraged, and worried.

He realized that on the fifth day he must kill a moose or fail in his mission for the journey back to the stronghold would require, at least, two days. Impatiently, he started searching for six large stones.

At length, Osseo found six that suited him. While he was stealthily creeping near his prey, he saw something shining in the coarse grass. When he picked up this sharp, diamond-shaped stone, blood started gushing from his hand. The stone had cut him. Osseo smiled, for the thought came to him that this sharp stone would kill the moose if only he could hit the animal's heart.

His high spirits soon gave way to seriousness when he

asked himself, "How can I be sure that the stone will go into the moose's hide at the right angle?" He pondered over this problem. He finally said to himself, "I'll tie the stone to a stick, that my aim may be more nearly accurate." As soon as Osseo found a suitable stick, he fastened the stone to the end with a piece of hide.

Then he practiced throwing the weapon into the trunk of a tree. Each time as he practiced, he moved back from it until the distance between him and the tree was equal to that between him and a moose. From this point, he threw the weapon but, although it hit the mark, it wouldn't stay in the tree. Again he realized that his lack of muscle was defeating him. His spirits sank lower with every failure. He couldn't bear to disappoint his father and to lose the respect of the tribe because of his weakness. He bit his lips to keep from weeping.

At last, completely discouraged, he threw himself upon the grass. "What shall I do?" What shall I do?" he moaned. At length, as he lay there, he noticed a small, curved branch lying nearby on the ground. He picked it up and examined it carefully. At last, an idea came. "Would it work?" he wondered. "No harm in trying," he told himself. And so Osseo tied a long narrow piece of hide to one end of the branch, pulled this stringlike piece as hard as he could, and fastened it to the other end of the branch. The figure resembled a half moon. Picking up the stone-tipped stick, he placed it on the hide. Then he drew back the hide as far as he could. When he let go, his weapon flew into the tree and stuck fast. Osseo hurried to the tree and after considerable difficulty, succeeded in removing the weapon. He practiced hitting the tree until his aim was practically perfect.

Then he looked for the moose that had wandered away. After sighting one, he walked as near to it as he dared, placed his weapon against the hide, and pulled the piece of hide toward him. He held the hide tightly while he aimed at the moose's heart. Then he let go. The weapon flew toward the moose, its mark, but lodged in the animal's neck. The wounded animal, stamping and pounding the earth, charged toward Osseo. Clouds of dust filled the air. For an instant, the young brave seemed frozen with fear and unable to move. Then, as the maddened animal with lowered head raised itself to strike, Osseo with lightninglike rapidity sent another sharp stone toward it. This time, the weapon hit its mark. The fatally wounded moose, with blood gushing from its wounds, fell to the ground. Then Osseo relaxed and smiled.

Remembering his father's instructions, he tied a piece of marked hide to the animal's leg for identification and put the weapon he had used beside the dead animal. Then Osseo hastened back to the stronghold. When he reached it, he hurried to the chief to announce his good news. The next day, the chief, two braves, and Osseo's father followed him to the spot where he had left the moose.

They were all amazed at Osseo's kill. They had not expected him to kill anything so big and powerful as a moose.

The chief spoke first. "This is good. How did you do it?"

Osseo bent over the moose, picked up the weapon, and took it to the chief. "With this, Great Chief," he said, putting the bow in the chief's hands. Then Osseo told the chief about his difficulty and how he had made the weapon.

As the chief listened, he exclaimed, "You are a courageous young brave. You may name the weapon."

Taking the branch with the hide on it, Osseo said, "I will call this branch a bow because it bent when I tied the hide on it." Picking up the stick tipped with the stone, he continued, "This weapon shall be known as an arrow in honor of our great goddess of wild nature, Arrometus."

Thereafter, the bow and arrow, which Osseo had made, became an essential part of Indian hunting and warfare, and Osseo was honored by the whole tribe.

Thirty

THE SUN CATCHER

Long, long ago, when Ayas was out hunting, he came to a trail in the woods where a fire had burned off all the thick undergrowth. Since Ayas had been tramping through the thicket all the forenoon, he began to feel tired. He lay down to rest on this spot that had been burned over. Soon he was fast asleep.

When Ayas woke up, he found that his deerskin coat, which he had thrown down nearby, had been chewed and torn. He was angry and cried out, "I'll find out who or what passed this place, and I'll punish the culprit for his mean trick." He immediately unstrung his bow and soon made a snare with his bow string, which had been made from dried deer sinew. Then he climbed a tall tree and set the trap on the highest branch and shouted, "I'll catch that squirrel and when I do—!" Without finishing his threat, Ayas went home.

But a queer thing happened. After supper, when it was time for night to come, it didn't get dark at all. Everybody

136

stood around waiting for nighttime, but the sun kept on shining. When the little children got sleepy and whined, their mothers wanted them to go to bed. But every child, even though he could scarcely keep his eyelids from drooping, said, "I can't go to bed when the sun is shining. Let me wait until it gets dark."

The raccoon, the skunk, the coyote, the fox, and all the other animals that hunt in the dark, began to howl. They were hungry, but they couldn't hunt any food in the daylight. In fact, everything was mixed up, but nobody knew what the trouble was. Ayas' sister thought her brother was to blame. She knew he was still angry about his damaged jacket. Finally, she said, "Ayas, you are always doing some mischief. What have you done this time? Do tell us."

Ayas only smiled. He seemed as puzzled as the other people. "Why doesn't it get dark?" he kept asking himself impatiently, for he liked to sit in the doorway of the wigwam every evening and listen to the noises that came from the woods.

Finally, the next day, Ayas said to his sister, "I set a trap yesterday. I am going to see whether I have caught anything." Soon Ayas reached the spot and found that the sun had been caught fast in his snare. It couldn't move across the sky! That was why there hadn't been any night.

Of course, all the animals were angry with Ayas. "You really fixed things up!" they said. "I suppose you know what will happen to us now. All of us will starve."

The animals gathered closer around Ayas and glared and snarled at him. Finally, the wolf said, "I think we should punish Ayas. He is always making trouble." The others agreed.

Ayas began to tremble for he was afraid of what the wolf and the others might do. He knew they were usually mean.

He was even more frightened when he thought what they might do when their stomachs were gnawing with hunger. Consequently, he began to plead with them.

"Now look here, I am just as sorry about this as you are," he said. "You know I wouldn't have trapped the sun on purpose. Please let me try to set him free."

After the animals had growled and threatened for some time, they agreed to let Ayas try. He hurried to the base of the tree and, fastening his arms tightly around the trunk, began to climb toward the top as fast as he could. But long before Ayas got there the heat of the sun burned him almost black, and he had to climb down faster than he went up. Then the skunk tried to climb up, but the heat through the limbs of the tree made stripes of black on his white coat. The mole lost his eyesight in his effort.

All the time the sun shone just as brightly as ever. The night-hunting animals grew more angry with Ayas every minute.

Soon the coyote gritted his teeth. "You'd better do something right away to get the sun loose or it will be too bad for you!" he hissed.

This threat made Ayas even more frightened than he had been before. He knew that the coyote meant business and wouldn't tolerate any delay. "Oh, I must think of something at once," he moaned. "Maybe the beaver could help!" As soon as the idea popped into his head, Ayas hurried down to a pond where the beaver was building a dam. "Oh, Beaver, come up and help me. Please gnaw down that tree yonder. It is the only way we can get the sun out of my snare," he urged.

The beaver, realizing the seriousness of the situation, soon came and with his sharp teeth began gnawing and gnawing at the big oak. In a short time, a bear woke up and hurried to see what was going on. As soon as he saw what the beaver was doing, he put a stop to the beaver's activity at once.

"If you cut down that tree and the sun falls to the earth, everything will burn up. The sun must not get any closer than he is," he warned.

Now, by this time, the whole settlement was alarmed. Everybody was racking his brains trying to think of some way to free the sun. Many tried but their efforts failed, either because the sun burned them or its bright light blinded them. It began to look as though the sun was there to stay.

Finally, a soft, furry, little animal came over to where

Ayas was sitting, hunched on the ground, and worrying about how to get the sun out of his snare. It was a mouse. He said, "Ayas, let me try to get the sun loose."

All the other animals began to laugh loudly at the mouse. "Everybody has tried and failed," they said. "What do you think a tiny creature like you can do?"

"Well," said the mouse, "my failure wouldn't be any worse than that of the others. Please let me try."

Finally, the animals agreed that although it wouldn't do any good, yet since it couldn't do any harm to anyone except the mouse, to let him try.

Almost immediately, the little mouse began gnawing at the string. It gnawed and gnawed for several days. Finally, the string broke and the sun started striding down its path to the western edge of the world. Soon night came and then daytime again just as it was supposed to do.

Then the night-hunting animals said to Ayas, "You'd better be careful where you set your trap after this. We are tired of your tricks. Next time, we won't let you off unpunished."

In a short time, everything was back to normal for everybody except the little mouse. The sun had scorched his soft skin and made it yellow. Ever since that time, certain types of mice have been yellow. Had it not been for the brave little mouse, the sun would have remained a prisoner, and the world would never again have had any of the blessings of night.

Thirty-one

FOUR WISHES FULFILLED

Many, many years ago, four Indian braves sat around a campfire during a powwow. They listened attentively and reverently as the old men recounted the brave deeds of their ancestors and their suffering of great hardships while they fought hostile tribes and enemies. At length, the braves said, "We, too, would help our people. Tell us what we can do." Some of the aged Indians offered suggestions, but none of their ideas pleased the young braves.

"Let us go to Manabozho," suggested one of the four. "The Great Manabozho will tell us what we can do."

His three companions looked up, startled. "Manabozho!" exclaimed the oldest. "No one has ever dared to go to him!"

"The Great One lives far away in the north country," added the third, shaking his head dubiously. "It is too far away and the way is filled with danger."

The fourth brave remained silent and gazed thoughtfully into the fire. At length, he spoke. "It is true that no moccasin has ever trodden the country of the great Manabozho.

141

No one has dared to approach the Great One. Yet these facts do not mean that we cannot go." The braves continued to smoke. Finally one leaped to his feet and exclaimed:

"Our brother is right. If we go, we shall be the first. To be the first to approach Manabozho will bring honor to us." His earnestness convinced the other braves.

Consequently, one fall day the four young braves departed full of hope, joy, and enthusiasm. They took with them some dried pumpkin, parched corn, and a small amount of dried venison. Upon the bushes berries grew, and fruit hung from the trees. But the way was hard and long. When winter came and snow and ice covered the ground and bushes, the braves could not find berries and green shoots. Their supply of food was soon exhausted. They were often hungry, for game was scarce. Cold benumbed their bodies and taxed their strength. As they journeyed, each day became more difficult; yet Manabozho's domain was still far off. Finally, one brave, discouraged, hungry, and homesick, said, "There is no use in our going farther. Let us return home."

But the other three reassured him and answered, "When Manabozho sees what we have suffered he will surely grant our wishes. Let us continue for a few moons longer."

At night, after they had made camp, the travellers tried to imagine what the home of Manabozho would look like. They felt sure that the wigwam would be large and made of the finest elk hide. The floor would be covered with bear- and sealskins. There would be an abundance of food and warm clothing. Many strong braves would do Manabozho's bidding. These thoughts aroused their hopes and made them quicken their steps.

One day, after months of weary travelling, the braves arrived at the base of a beautiful mountain covered with gleaming snow. Nearby, they noticed a small hut. "Let's stop there to ask the way to Manabozho's," suggested the oldest brave. Just imagine their surprise when a man clothed in bearskin stood in the doorway and said, "Welcome, come rest and eat. Well, I know that you have come to ask for some wish that you cherish dearly or you would never have travelled so far and endured such hardships."

"'Tis he!" exclaimed the braves as they dropped upon their faces. Manabozho bade them rest while he prepared food for them.

After the braves had eaten and rested, they felt refreshed and were grateful that their long journey was over. They soon told Manabozho of their hardships. When they had given an account of their long journey, Manabozho said, "I am well pleased with you, young braves. Tell me your mission."

Then the oldest brave spoke first, as was the custom. "I wish to live long that I may help my people. I have seen them die of fever. I would that I might bring relief and healing to them."

"You shall indeed," said Manabozho. "Go and stand beside the river." The brave ran eagerly to the edge of the water and there he was changed into a tall graceful cedar. Its seeds were spread by the north winds. Great forests sprung from them. In time, these trees gave shelter to animals and men. Hunters often used the boughs of the cedar for a bed when they were forced to spend the night in the woods. Its bark was used to cure fever, and its roots for making baskets. Soon the Indians began to count the cedar as one of their greatest blessings.

Then the second brave bowed before the Great Spirit and spoke anxiously, "I, too, want to help my people. I have seen them suffer from lack of warmth and food."

143

Manabozho smiled. "You shall become a great granite mountain. Hereafter, men shall use stones from your quarries for spearheads, hammers, and flint to kindle fire for heat and cooking. You shall provide stones to build beautiful homes and temples. You shall give stone of lasting endurance and beauty to all mankind."

Hearing what Manabozho had done for his companions, the third asked to be heard. "I have seen my people toil to sow the grain and then later have the green shoots wither and die because of drought. I have seen the streams dry up and man die of thirst."

"Go," said Manabozho, "to the mountain top afar." The brave immediately set out. When he reached the top, he was changed to the great rain god. Then the clouds formed; the lightning flashed and the thunder roared; rain fell upon the land and swelled the streams and rivers which were filled with fish. "Man cannot live without rain to produce crops and fill the streams," Manabozho explained to the last brave. "When the Indians hear the thunderous voice of your friend, they will be very grateful."

The fourth brave, seeing how great his friends had become, was filled with wonder and amazement. What could he ask that would be of great service? He was puzzled and perplexed.

"And you?" said Manabozho, addressing the brave. "Have you no wish?"

The fourth brave was silent for a long time. He wondered and then said again to himself, "Who will see the beautiful cedar tree and remember that it once was a brave, or who will look upon the granite hill and know that a brave Indian is at its heart, or who in the years to come will recognize the presence of my friend in the thunder, lightning, and

rain? No, these are not enough. I must have something greater for my people than these."

After some time, he raised his head and faced the Great One. "O Manabozho," he exclaimed, "many tribes beset our nation on every side. I would like to be the greatest war chief in my village."

"Go home! Your wish shall be granted," exclaimed Manabozho. "Your name shall be one that will spread fear into the hearts of other warriors and courage to many of the oppressed. Your war club shall speak loudly. Your belt shall be hung with trophies and your hair decorated with eagle feathers. All men shall honor you!"

145

For many days, the brave travelled homeward. At length, weary and footsore, he reached his village. There his people were anxiously waiting news of him and the three other braves.

After he had eaten, he commanded that smoke signals and drums should summon the tribes to a meeting at which he would tell them what had happened. Then he lay down in his wigwam and slept.

Soon the neighboring tribes came and gathered around a huge fire. Then the brave told them of the wishes of the three braves and what Manabozho had done for them. The chiefs nodded approvingly and then a young warrior asked, "Pray, what was your wish?"

The brave hesitated for a moment, straightened his shoulders and said proudly, "I asked to be the greatest war chief in my village and my wish was granted!" Then, grasping several arrows from his belt, he broke them into halves. "What does this mean?" cried several of the warriors.

"It means," said the Great Chief, "that no longer will arrows be used to wound and kill others. They shall be used to kill only the animals that we need for food. Each of us should have a purpose and a goal. Mine shall be to work for a lasting peace for all mankind. Let us work together and live in harmony, following the example of the great Manabozho."

Lighting the peace pipe, the Great Chief took a puff and handed it to a chief near him. Then each chief and each warrior in turn smoked this sacred pipe and pledged his honor never again to kill his brothers or fight another tribe. To keep that lasting peace the brave's descendants are still striving.

Trees That Grow So Fair

Thirty-two

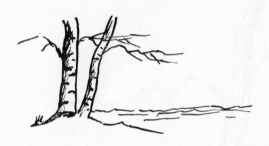

WHY BIRCHES HAVE SCARS

One fall day as Manabozho was strolling among the white birches along the lake shore, he saw something strange approaching him. He wondered what it could be. As soon as Manabozho was close enough, he saw that the strange object was a large black bear. Now Manabozho knew that this animal would be a formidable foe and so he quickly pulled up a young tree by the roots and then hid and waited to kill this approaching enemy. When it was close by, Manabozho jumped from his hiding place. Striking the bear on the head with the uprooted tree, Manabozho killed it with one blow.

In spite of the fact that Manabozho did not like bear meat, for it was often tough, he decided to roast the animal, because he was hungry. He built a fire, and as soon as it had burned down a bit, he held the bear over the coals to singe off its fur. When he had done it, he cut up the bear's body and set it roasting. By this time, Manabozho had some sharp pains in his stomach. He was really hungry and wanted his dinner as soon as possible.

While Manabozho was waiting for his dinner to cook, he heard a strange noise which, at first, he was unable to locate. After searching carefully, he discovered that a strong wind was rubbing two tree tops together. This noise made Manabozho nervous. At last, he exclaimed, "I can stand this

150

disturbance no longer." Even though he was eating his dinner at the time, he felt that he must stop the noise at once. Leaving his meal on the ground, Manabozho climbed one of the trees. He soon reached the spot where the trees rubbed together. He tried to pull them apart, but while he struggled, his hand became wedged between the limbs. He pulled and pulled, but he could not get his hand free.

Now while Manabozho was held prisoner in the tree top, he heard a pack of hungry wolves that had smelled the roasting meat and had come to get it. In spite of his shouts, they soon ate the roasted bear greedily. Poor Manabozho couldn't stop them! They paid no attention to his cries and threats. For some time, although Manabozho tugged and tugged to free his hand, he was unable to do so. But at last, after a hard jerk, he managed to get free. When he climbed down as fast as he could, for he was starved, he found that the wolves had eaten every scrap of the bear except its skull. Manabozho was very angry. How he longed to punish the thieves! But they had fled and so, of course, he realized that they were out of his reach. Therefore, the enraged Manabozho decided to punish the white birches instead. He resolved to do it so severely that they would never squeeze his hand again. He hurried to get a big, strong whip. As soon as he found one that was sufficiently strong, he beat the trees with all his strength.

Now until that time, the white birches had been the most beautiful trees in all the woods. The Indians often called them the ghosts of the forest. Their slender trunks had been snow-white and perfectly smooth without any scratches or blemishes. But after Manabozho had whipped them unmercifully, their creamy white bark became covered with tan or dark-brown spots. Ever since, these graceful trees have borne the ugly scars of that terrible beating.

Thirty-three

WHY THE EVERGREEN TREES
NEVER LOSE THEIR LEAVES

When the winds became cold and the days grew gray and shorter, all the birds flew far to the South where the breezes were warm, and where they could find insects and berries to eat. Did I say all the birds? No, one little bird had broken its wing and could not fly with the others. It was left all alone in the North in the cold and snow. At first, the poor creature did not know what to do. After a while, since the forest looked warm, it hopped, as well as it could, to the trees there to ask for shelter.

First, it came to a birch tree. "Beautiful Birch Tree," it said, "my wing is broken and my friends have flown away to the Southland. May I live among your branches until my friends come back to me in the spring?"

"No, indeed!" exclaimed the Birch Tree, drawing her branches closer to her. "We in this forest have our own birds to care for. I can do nothing for you."

"The Birch seemed unfriendly," thought the little bird

to itself. "Maybe it isn't strong and couldn't hold me when the North Wind blows. I shall ask a sturdy oak."

So the crippled bird said, "Great Oak Tree, you can see that I have a broken wing. Since you are so strong, will you let me live in your branches until my friends come back in the spring?"

"It will be a long time until spring!" cried the Oak. "You would get hungry and eat my acorns. No, I can't help you. I do all that I can when I feed the squirrels."

"It may be that the beech will help me," thought the poor bird and it said, "Beautiful Beech, I love your smooth grey bark. Will you let me lodge in your branches till springtime? Because my wing was broken, I could not fly to the South with the other birds."

"No, I cannot be bothered with you," said the tall Beech. "I have not yet recovered from the confusion and noise which the people made in gathering my nuts. Leave me in peace."

"Possibly the gentle willow will be kind to me," thought the bird, and it said, "Gentle Willow, I have been seriously injured. My right wing was broken. I could not fly when the other birds went to the warm South. May I have shelter in your branches until spring?"

The Willow did not look gentle. Haughtily, she exclaimed, "Willows never talk to people whom they do not know. We have never met. Doubtless, there are trees that will take in strange birds. I'll appreciate it if you will leave me at once."

The poor little bird did not know what to do or where to go. Its wing was not yet strong, but it tried to hop away as best it could. It had not gone far before it heard a voice say, "Little Bird, where are you going?"

"I do not know," answered the little bird. "I am very cold, and my wing is almost frozen."

"Come right here, then," said the friendly Spruce, for she was the one who had called. "You may live on my warmest branch all winter if you choose."

"Oh, may I?" asked the little bird happily.

"Indeed you may!" answered the kindhearted Spruce. "If your friends have flown, it is time that the trees offered their assistance. Here is a branch where my leaves are thickest."

"My branches are not very thick," said the friendly Pine, "but I am tall and strong and can protect you and the Spruce when the North Wind blusters."

"I can help too," said the Juniper. "I can give you berries

154

all winter. All the birds know that juniper berries are very good."

And so the Spruce gave the crippled bird a warm branch; the Pine protected it from the stormy blasts; and the Juniper gave it berries to eat.

The other trees were angered by the actions of the friendly trees. They said haughtily, "We are particular about the friends we choose!"

During the night, a terrible storm arose. The cold North Wind blew very hard. Every leaf that it touched fell from the tree. Soon the birch, the oak, the beech, and the willow trees were almost bare.

"May I destroy every leaf in the forest?" asked the North Wind joyously.

"No," replied the Great Spirit. "The trees that have been kind to the little bird with the broken wing may keep their leaves."

For that reason, the leaves of the spruce, the pine, and the juniper are always green.

Thirty-four

WHY PINE TREES WEEP

The Chippewas believed that Mongo was the first man to live upon the earth, and that he came from the land of the rising sun. He chose to make his home among the rivers of the North, and on the shores of the Great Lakes. Although the rivers and lakes were filled with fish, and the woods with game, Mongo found little pleasure in fishing and hunting for he was unhappy and discontented. He had no companion with whom to share his joys and sorrows. The Great Spirit realized that he was lonesome and sad.

One night, Mongo sat in front of his wigwam warming himself by a big campfire. His heart was unusually heavy. While he sat grieving, he was suddenly startled by a bright light in the heavens. As he looked up, he saw a beautiful star falling swiftly toward the earth with a train of bright flames following in its path. The brilliant ball fell almost at Mongo's feet, and when it burst into many pieces, a stately woman, beautiful as the dawn, stood before him.

Mongo was exceedingly frightened and embarrassed. He would have run away, but this lovely woman smiled and held out her hand. She beckoned for him to come to her,

and then told him her name was Wasqua, which means newborn light. They talked of many things which interested both of them. At length, Mongo forgot his fears. He felt very happy, for he had found a friend. Soon love filled his heart and he led his lovely Wasqua to his wigwam where for many moons they lived happily together. With Wasqua, Mongo once again found pleasure in fishing and hunting. They had several children for whom Wasqua made deerskin clothing trimmed with beads and feathers. As a family, they loved each other devotedly.

One day, Mongo became ill. Wasqua nursed him tenderly and gave him the medicine which she had prepared, but in spite of her careful nursing, Mongo grew steadily worse and died in a short time.

Wasqua, filled with sorrow because of the death of her husband, lay upon Mongo's grave and wept. In spite of the effort of her friends, she refused to leave his grave. She put aside the food which the animals and birds brought to her. At night, bears and wolves lay down by her side to keep her warm. Still she grieved and fasted. Day after day went by. Gradually Wasqua's strength began to fail. Every day she grew weaker. At length, just at sunset, faithful Wasqua was laid in a grave by the side of her husband. The whippoorwill's voice was hushed, and the wolf's howl echoed throughout the forest, so great was the grief of all living creatures.

But before the sun shone on that grave again, a great pine, like a solitary sentinel, stood at the head of the graves where the first man and his wife were buried. The pine was the first of its kind among the trees of the forest. Night and day, it wept and sang a sweet, sad song over the lonely graves. Even to this day, the pine trees sigh, moan, and weep for the first-born of the earth.

Pine trees easily gather moisture which slides off the needles in the form of rain. The Chippewas believe that this moisture is Wasqua's tears which she shed on Mongo's grave.

Because My Love Has Come

Thirty-five

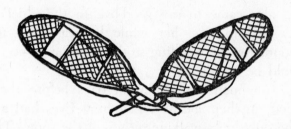

THE SNOWSHOES

Laughing Eyes, the beautiful daughter of Chief Pemige-wasset, had two young suitors. One was Wasawa whom Laughing Eyes and all the Indians liked. The other was Oakana whom the chief admired more than he did Wasawa. Because Chief Pemigewasset did not want to make his daughter unhappy by choosing her husband arbitrarily himself, he tried to think of some way to persuade or influence her to marry Oakana. At last, he thought of a plan.

Now at this time, Chief Pemigewasset had a message which he wished to send to a chief in the far North. He sent for Wasawa and Oakana and said to them, "I have prepared two copies of a message that I want taken to a chief in the faraway Northland. Each of you may carry one of them. The brave who returns with a reply first may have Laughing Eyes for his wife." Chief Pemigewasset knew it would be a difficult journey. The snow lay in deep drifts and there were no trees blazed to show the trail. Yet the suitors consented gladly, for each one felt he would be the successful one.

One day, a short time before Wasawa was ready to leave,

161

he came to see Laughing Eyes. This handsome, young brave found her very unhappy because she realized that Wasawa was not so strong as Oakana. Wasawa comforted her and told her that he felt sure he could win the race. His rival, Oakana, also came to say good-bye to the chief's lovely daughter and to urge her while he was gone to make preparations for the wedding so that as soon as he returned they could be married.

Now it happened that several days before the young braves left on their journey, Laughing Eyes had a dream. In it, she saw ducks walking on top of the snow. Then she awoke. After a while she fell asleep again, and dreamed that she saw even more ducks gliding along on the top of the snow. A third time, she fell asleep and again dreamed that she saw ducks on top of the snowbank, but the other birds attempting to do so sank down into the deep snow. Laughing Eyes had been taught to believe in dreams, but she was puzzled over her dreams and their meaning. She felt sure that they must have something to do with the journey that her suitors were to make.

All her life, Laughing Eyes had loved the animals and birds. The thought of their being cold and hungry worried her. All winter she had been scattering food in front of her wigwam for them. Two ducks had stayed there during the winter weather instead of flying to the South with their companions. They came to feed with the other birds. They were so tame that Laughing Eyes could go very close to them. She caught one of the ducks and threw it far out over the snow. She did it several times and each time, the duck ran back to her. The girl caught another bird and threw it in the same way, but this bird sank down in the snow. Laughing Eyes had to rescue it. Her dream began to have meaning.

162

Laughing Eyes examined the feet of the birds carefully. She soon saw that the web between the toes of the ducks enabled them to walk on the snow. She went into her wigwam to think. After a while, she took a roll of soft deer skin, and some pliable strips of ash which her father used for making bows. After she had cut thongs from the deerskin, she bent a strip of wood into a frame and fastened it firmly together. Then she fastened other strips of skin to the frame with which to tie on the shoe. After she had finished one, she made another.

When Wasawa came to say good-bye, Laughing Eyes told him of her dream and showed him the shoes which she felt sure would serve the same purpose as the webbed feet on the duck. At first, Wasawa only laughed at the queer-looking objects and made fun of them. Laughing Eyes was hurt by Wasawa's attitude. Then she said earnestly, "O Wasawa, please try the shoes for my sake. I want you to get back quickly and safely. The journey will be long and difficult. I shall be worried until I see you again." Moved by her pleading, Wasawa agreed to try them. Then she asked him not to show the shoes to anyone else and not to let Oakana see him put them on. Wasawa quickly promised Laughing Eyes, for he felt sure that if these strange shoes were seen, the beholder would ridicule and humiliate him.

Finally, the day arrived for the suitors' departure. Just before these young braves were ready to set forth on this long and difficult journey, Chief Pemigewasset gave them the two messages which he had painted on a roll of birch bark. The young men set out together. All the Indians watched them leave and hoped that Wasawa would win. However, they did not think that he could.

The snow was deep and the North Wind with its icy blast whipped them constantly all day long. The second day, more snow fell in great drifts. Walking became even more difficult. Oakana, who was very strong, soon left Wasawa far behind. Then Wasawa took out the snow shoes, which, wrapped in a skin, he had carried on his back. He fastened them on, tried to walk, but soon muttered, "No good!" However, he had promised Laughing Eyes that he would not throw the shoes away until he had given them a fair trial. Some distance away, he saw a tree. He decided to wear the snowshoes until he reached it. It took him a long while. He had many falls, but by the time he reached his goal, he realized that he had not once sunk down into the deep, soft snow. "Perhaps these shoes are worth something after all," he said to himself. He continued to wear them and soon found that by doing so he could keep his footing more easily. He soon was able to walk much faster than previously. Finally, he tried running, and by sundown, he was able to race over the snow.

One evening, after several weeks of hardships and suffering with cold, Wasawa came to the Indian village where he was to deliver the message. He soon found the chief's lodge. The chief was watching the sunset when Wasawa arrived. The rays of the dying sun had cast a beautiful glow on the bright snow. The chief took the message, but he did not open it. However, he looked sharply at the messenger's feet as he set food before him.

The snowshoes continued to hold the chief's attention and within a few days all the tribe had come to look at Wasawa's feet. Contrary to their custom, the Indians began asking questions and showing their curiosity. "Where did you get the moccasins? Who made them? Why did you wear them? What good are they?" questioned the Indians. Wasawa had to explain all about his strange shoes.

Wasawa stayed and rested a few days while the chief

prepared an answer to Chief Pemigewasset's message. At last, the young brave was ready to return home. When he left, many of the tribe followed him part of the way on snow shoes for the squaws had been very busy copying his shoes.

One day, Chief Pemigewasset heard the cry, "Wasawa is

coming! Wasawa is back!" The Chief only smiled. He realized that the young brave would have done very well had he been able to reach the village in the far North by this time. But soon, Wasawa entered Chief Pemigewasset's wigwam and said, "I have brought back the answer to your message."

Chief Pemigewasset could scarcely believe his eyes when he saw Wasawa standing before him! The chief immediately thought that the young brave was trying to deceive him. However, as soon as the chief saw the pictures on the scroll, he knew that Wasawa had told the truth. Immediately, he gave orders for the preparation of a grand wedding feast for Laughing Eyes and Wasawa. The whole village rejoiced with Wasawa and his beautiful dark-eyed bride.

When Oakana arrived at the village in the North, the chief said, "I received this same message some time ago. I sent my answer back several moons ago with a young brave named Wasawa who had wings on his feet."

Thirty-six

SNOWBIRD

Within the shadow of a mountain of gleaming quartzite, many years ago, there lived a beautiful maiden, the daughter of an Indian chief. When she was only a few months old, her parents had named her Snowbird. Each year, Snowbird had seemed to grow more beautiful. By the time she had become a young woman, suitors vied with one another to win her favor.

Throughout her childhood, Snowbird had wanted to climb to the summit of the beautiful mountain, but to reach the highest peak, towering one thousand feet, had been too strenuous for her strength. Again and again as she grew older, Snowbird, accompanied by her friends, strove to reach the summit, but the party always failed. Yet Snowbird refused to accept defeat and at last, when she was sixteen, she accomplished her desire.

After this feat, Snowbird was courted by many braves. When her father, Chief Bald Eagle, recognized the persistence of the suitors, he called a council of the braves.

Dressed in the tribal costume of deerskin, beautifully

167

embroidered with beads and colorful porcupine quills, and wearing a magnificent headdress of upright, overlapping eagle feathers, held in position by a wide beaded band, he said with great dignity and deliberation:

"The coming of spring has aroused in my only daughter feelings of love. All around me, I see many suitors who would gladly wed this beautiful girl, but only seven have had the courage to risk their lives to woo her." As he spoke, his piercing eyes settled on the embarrassed young warriors.

"Of all our tribe, Snowbird alone has climbed that lofty peak," he continued proudly. Immediately following his gesture, the eyes of all the suitors turned toward the gleaming mountain. "Snowbird will climb the crag again today. If one of the suitors can follow her to the summit, he may win her and later take my place as chief of the tribe."

A glance at Snowbird's big dark eyes, copper-colored skin, long black braids, and winning smile readily inflamed the hearts of the seven warriors. The contest began at once. Each brave was determined to win the prize.

Soon seven suitors were following Snowbird as she climbed the rocky cliff. After climbing for some time, two of the braves became exhausted and were forced to turn back. At the halfway mark, another suitor gave up, and a bit higher up the crag, a fourth fell. He was rescued by a fifth brave. These two, convinced that further efforts would be futile, returned to the base of the cliff. The two remaining suitors continued to climb and struggled to maintain a foothold on the slippery, bare peak. At last, the weaker one slipped, and fell on the sharp crags hundreds of feet below.

Snowbird nearly fell as she glanced down upon the last brave clinging desperately to the steep, almost perpendicular wall of the cliff. Slowly, the beautiful maiden and her persistent suitor continued upward. Finally Snowbird reached the top. Within a few inches of the goal, the exhausted brave missed his foothold, but clung to the rock with swollen, bleeding hands, as his body dangled over the side of the mountain. He couldn't possibly go any farther. "Alas," thought Snowbird, "he is weak like the others. No one is strong and worthy enough to be my husband and the chief of my people. Let his weakness bring about his death."

Turning away, Snowbird gazed across the glittering peak. As she looked, a great loneliness such as she had never known before crept over her. "Where am I to find," she asked herself, "a man as strong and courageous as the brave hovering near death just below me? He has risked his life for my sake." At that moment, she realized that she loved this brave.

Quickly, she hurried to the edge of the precipice, reached down, and helped the exhausted lover to safety. Without further delay, he claimed the lovely maiden for his wife, and later upon the death of Bald Eagle, he became the chief of the tribe.

Thirty-seven

SAWGAMO'S DAUGHTER

The Indians still talk in whispers of Sawgamo, a mighty Manito, who had a daughter of unusual beauty. When she was born, no name other than Belle seemed suitable for this lovely child. Indeed she was so very beautiful that Sawgamo feared that someone might kidnap her. He vowed that he would immediately destroy anyone who attempted to take her from him.

When she was only a child, Sawgamo taught Belle the secrets of the forests, the skies, and the waters. She discovered the haunts of the fleet-footed deer, the beaver, and the opossum; she learned to use nature's brightest dyes for her head bands and garments. Sawgamo showed Belle that everything in the world was governed by certain laws. The sun, the moon, and the sea were obedient to the Manitoes that guided them. Thus he taught Belle that she must be obedient to him lest some harm come to her. Like all Indian girls, Belle listened to her father's instruction and obeyed his wishes. When strangers came, she appeared preoccupied or else slipped away into the forest.

Sawgamo watching her one evening, as she cooked their evening meal, realized that his daughter would soon be a young woman. She had seemed to grow more beautiful with each passing day. She was as slender and graceful as a willow, her hair was long and black, her lips were the color of luscious raspberries and her eyes were dark and luminous. At this time, Sawgamo became anxious, for he feared that Belle might fall in love. Already rumors of Belle's unusual beauty had spread throughout the land of the Chippewas. Many strong warriors had come to Sawgamo's wigwam to see this beautiful maiden and for a pretext had asked her father, "When is the moon for the Great Hunt? Where is the beaver's lodge?"

The great Manito's fears continued to mount day by day. The thought that he might lose his beautiful daughter filled him with continuous anxiety. He felt that he could no longer take the risk of losing her. He pondered over what would be the best thing to do and at last devised a plan.

For several days, Sawgamo worked busily cutting birch bark, gathering pitch, and picking out his finest and strongest sinews which he twisted into a strong rope.

One day, Belle wandered down to the shore where her father was working. "O Wise Father," she asked, as she looked at a strange box he was building of birch bark, "what is this beautiful box you are making?"

"Come, see, my fair one," said her father gently. "Do you not think this box would be a lovely place in which to live? I am building this box strong and firm and waterproof." In this way, Belle found out that the box was being made for her and that her father intended it to be her home thereafter. Sawgamo had decided that if she were hidden in

172

a box floating on the water but fastened securely to the shore that no one would see her; consequently, he would never lose her. Soon the box was finished.

Belle did not dislike her new home; in fact, she quite enjoyed it for the waves rocked the box gently. Day after day, Belle floated on the deep blue water and played with the fish that swam around her. Finally, after moons and moons of inactivity, Belle grew restless and lonely. "Surely my father will not mind if I come closer to the shore that I may speak with him," she murmured. Almost the next moment, she started to put her thoughts into action. She pulled on the thong of sinew until the box floated very near to the forest-covered shore. There she waited to gain her father's permission to leave her home on the water and go into the wigwam.

While she tarried, a young dark-haired brave came hurrying toward the lake, carrying a handful of beautiful flowers. She looked at him with surprise and thought that she had never before seen a man so young and handsome. When the brave saw this beautiful maiden he gasped with admiration and exclaimed, "Who are you, O lovely maiden?"

"I am Belle, Sawgamo's daughter. I live in this birchbark box where my father has hidden me from the braves who would try to steal me. But who are you, happy stranger?"

"I am South Wind, bearer of blue skies, fruit, flowers, and everything fresh and green. Wherever I am, life is happy and gay; yet I would be very much happier if you would be my wife."

Then dark-eyed Belle answered sadly, "I cannot grant your wish, for my father has vowed that no one shall have me for his wife. I cannot disobey my father."

Since South Wind had fallen deeply in love with Belle, he decided to remain on shore that he might be near her. While he lingered, the trees put on their most gorgeous gowns of red, russet, and gold, and Indian summer prevailed. While the days were sunny and bright, South Wind continued to tell Belle of the joys and pleasures he would give her if she would be his bride. Thus he loved and wooed her, but the beautiful girl sadly shook her head and said, "Father will never break his vow."

At length, a chilling breeze blew from the north, and

174

South Wind began to tremble. Soon the fields were bare and brown, the autumn leaves became sere and fell from the boughs, the flowers drooped and died, freezing blasts blew from the leadened skies, and the pines groaned and swayed. Then a powerful young brave came whistling through the tree tops and alighted between Belle, who was seated in her birch-bark home, and South Wind, who rested on the shore.

"I am the all-powerful North Wind. It is I who sweep everything before me, bring the ice and snow, and kill all growing things everywhere," he shouted boastfully. On seeing Belle and being fascinated by her unusual beauty, he exclaimed, "Who are you, lovely maiden, in your strange box? Who are you, young brave, with the withered flowers in your hand?"

"I am South Wind, the king of summer. This beautiful girl is Belle, the daughter of Sawgamo, whom many moons I have wooed, for I am determined to have her for my lovely bride!"

"Your sovereignty is over, South Wind, for you have waited too long and have grown pale and powerless. Those flowers in your hand withered and froze at the first touch of my icy breath. This beautiful girl shall be my own bride!" exclaimed the blusterer with a roar.

Then North Wind challenged South Wind to a duel and as they fought, a terrific storm arose. The winds howled and whistled, the sky shook, the thunder roared, the lightning flashed across the sky, and black rain and hail whipped the earth. During the gale, Belle's home broke loose from its moorings. As the birch-bark box was buffeted and tossed about, the frightened girl screamed for help, but the storm drowned her cries. For hours, this box was carried and tossed about by the fury of the gales. Finally, it was catapulted on

175

the shore of an island belonging to the Prophet, the keeper of the Gates of the Lakes.

After the storm had abated, the Prophet noticing the strange boat hurried to see what it might be. He was surprised indeed to find a young woman with a tear-stained face, soggy clothes, and wet hair asleep in the birch-bark box. She looked so very weary and completely exhausted that he sat down by the box to wait until she awoke. When Belle slowly opened her eyes and saw the strange face, she wept and was frightened.

"Do not fear me, lovely maiden, for I shall never harm you. From whence have you come and how did you happen to be out on the water in that terrible storm and in such a strange boat?"

Then Belle told the Prophet of South Wind's wooing, of the North Wind's challenge to the South Wind for a duel, of the battered condition of the box, and finally of its being loosened from its moorings and being dashed by the storm and waves upon the island. Then the Prophet quickly brought Belle some food. As she ate, she continued the story and told him of her father Sawgamo and his strange vow.

Then the Prophet, who had loved Belle from the moment he first saw her, said, "Your father will never find you, for the shores of the Great Lakes are long and irregular. I do not fear Sawgamo. You shall be my lovely bride." Since she loved the Prophet, they were married very soon.

The Prophet and Belle were exceedingly happy on their island, but their happiness was not to last very long. For as soon as the storm had subsided, Sawgamo hastened to try to recover his daughter and to search the shores of Lake Huron and explore every inlet and bay. Finally, he found Belle and her husband in their island home.

Sawgamo was filled with rage when he realized that the

176

Prophet had married Belle. Stretching out his arms toward the heavens, he shouted, "You have taken my beautiful daughter and now you shall be punished. Let all the forces of nature combine to destroy this robber and the island on which he stands." Immediately, a terrific storm followed. The land on which the Prophet and his bride were standing was torn and tossed into a myriad of small pieces. The ground where Belle was started floating rapidly down the lake. The Prophet seeing his wife's plight jumped into the lake and swam toward her. But alas, he could not overtake her and he drowned. The island on which Belle stood floated into the Saint Clair and Detroit Rivers. There her father found her. He decided to let her stay on this island forever. To protect her and to avoid further trouble, he put rattlesnakes on the island. Since that time, the poisonous serpents have disappeared, and the beautiful island, now known as Belle Isle, has become a spacious park and picnic ground for the people living in Detroit.

Why Birds Do Sing

Thirty-eight

THE ORIGIN OF THE BIRDS

The Great Spirit enjoyed the sun, the moon, the sky, and the stars, but most of all he loved earth's growing things. Day after day, he watched the flowers and the trees grow, but he was not satisfied, for he wanted more trees. Finally, one day he exclaimed, "Wherever my foot touches the ground, let trees grow in abundance." Now the Great Spirit could do whatever he willed; therefore, at his command, maples, oaks, elms, pines, fruit trees, hemlocks, beeches, palms, and willows sprang up all over the earth. Then the Great Spirit sent gentle rain and warm sunshine to make the young trees grow. Every spring, he watched the budding shoots burst into beautiful leaves that later fanned the earth and shaded the ground. Soon squirrels and raccoons played in the branches of the trees and made their homes in them. After a while, beautiful apples and other fruits hung on the boughs of some of the trees. In autumn, the Great Spirit watched the fruit and the crops ripen, and the leaves turn scarlet, bright yellow, and brown.

Now in the North Country there lived a destructive spirit

called the Frost King. He had a powerful touch. Very soon after the fruit, the corn, and the pumpkins had been harvested, the North Wind with his freezing breath and the Frost King with icy finger tips came, sometimes even without any warning, and touched the wild grapes, the nuts, and all other growing things. The vines withered. One after another, the leaves fell from the beeches, the maples, the birches, the willows, and the oaks. Some leaves fell quickly; some fluttered and danced through the air, and others died slowly. However, over a few of the trees the North Wind and the Frost King had no power. When they came, these trees only laughed, swayed, and creaked. Some of them even boasted and said, "You cannot harm us; we are strong; the Frost King's icy fingers cannot hurt us." These were the spruce, the fir, the hemlock, the cedar, and the pine. Nevertheless, the North Wind was not discouraged and continued to blow the dead and sere leaves from the other trees; in a short time, their branches looked bare and desolate.

Every autumn, the Great Spirit sorrowed and grieved that so much beauty had been destroyed. Throughout the cold, hard winter he often pondered on how he might keep the leaves with him.

Now at that time, there were no little forest birds upon the earth, for the Great Spirit had not created them. There were only the birds that dwelt near the sea, like the sea gull, the wild duck, the loon, and the kingfisher. The North Wind and the Frost King had no power over them. These birds only mocked the Frost King and the North Wind and flew away and found refuge among the rocks or the reeds and in the thick grass of the marshland when they were pursued by these spirits. Then, too, there were some sturdy birds that were useful to man because they provided him with meat and eggs. These were hen, wild turkey, duck

and goose. Some of them could not fly very well; in fact, several merely waddled along. Their songs were only a quack and a cackle.

One winter day, the Great Spirit appeared very sad. He pondered deeply and was silent for a long time. At last, a smile spread over his face. He had hit upon a plan. He said, "I cannot restore to the trees the leaves which the Frost King has killed and stripped off, for it is too late. But I will take the fallen leaves and change them into little birds!"

As soon as the Great Spirit blew upon the brown and withered oak leaves, they were changed into tiny wrens with bright, cinnamon-brown backs, paler breasts and wings, and tails heavily barred with black. They looked very pert with their stubby tails standing erect over their backs. They hid in small piles of brush and sang with a rippling flow of melody.

Then the Great Spirit created the wood thrushes with reddish-brown backs, bright heads, and white breasts spotted heavily with black. These large birds, about eight inches long, love the swamps and moist woods. They are excellent songsters whose tones are very high and flute-like. They prefer to sing at night. The mockingbird, the next creation, proved to be a great vocalist. He lives in pastures, gardens, and open woods. Sometimes his song is sweet and pleasing, and at other times, harsh and unmusical. He loves to imitate the notes of the other birds. His ability makes them jealous.

Later, the Great Spirit touched the red and brown leaves. Immediately, robins with reddish-brown breasts flew about the trees whistling a loud, cheery carol, "Cheerily cheer up, cheerily cheer up," almost continuously. The red maple leaves were changed into scarlet tanagers that live in open woods, but often come to orchards and ploughed fields where they can feed on berries, seeds, and insects.

When the Great Spirit saw a heap of bright-yellow leaves lying on the ground, he transformed them into goldfinches, sometimes known as thistle birds, because they are often seen on thistles. They make their nests from thistle down.

184

Some of the brightest yellow leaves became brilliantly plumaged orioles. Pea-green parrots with their shrill voices were originally the few green leaves that had been left on the trees.

Last of all, the Great Spirit breathed upon the dead and gray leaves. When his breath touched these leaves, larks that make their grass nests on the ground became friends of the hillside and field. Perched on a treetop, they sing with clear, fife-like whistles. Sad to relate, the sparrows became fighters and bullies. These strong creatures are able to stand cold and hardship. Few of the other birds will live in the neighborhood with them. They commence to sing with harsh tones early in the morning and continue until night.

When the Great Spirit had finished his work, he waved his hand. Immediately great flocks of little birds twittered and sang in a great chorus. Their gorgeous plumage resembled the beautiful colors of the leaves that had given them birth. Rejoicing in his creation, the Great Spirit said, "I will give them power to fly through the air, to rest upon the air like a leaf fluttering, and to build their nests among the branches of the trees and shrubs or in the grass of the meadows. Although the Frost King will strip the trees of their leaves in the autumn, I will give the trees power to put forth new leaves every spring so that when summer comes, the branches will not be bare."

Looking about at his latest creation and hearing their sweet songs, the Great Spirit exclaimed, "Indeed, I am well pleased! I wish now for a bird of happiness to lead the birds to warm countries away from the ice and snow, and to bring them back here in the spring, for their songs delight me."

Almost instantly a beautiful, gentle bluebird soared out of the blue sky and seemed to warble continuously, "See, see, I'm here!"

185

Why Birds Do Sing

And so, when the winds become bitter cold, and the sky is covered with leaden clouds, the birds, following the bluebird, fly away to a warm country filled with flowers and sunshine, but return in the spring to gladden the woods and the fields with their songs.

Thirty-nine

THE BOLD FISH DUCK

In the fall of the year when the ducks began migrating to the Southland, a fish duck said to the other ducks, "No, I'm not going with you. Instead I intend to build myself a winter home in the rushes along the shore of the lake."

Soon he was busy building his nest. When he had finished it, he brought four logs to his home for fire wood. Each log would burn a month. Provided with four, he felt sure he could keep warm throughout the cold winter.

This fish duck was hearty and fearless. Even on the coldest days when the North Wind blew with icy blasts, this fearless creature would break the ice. Then he would swim and dive under the ice for food. Each day, he brought strings of fish to his nest.

One day, the North Wind, noticing the duck's action, decided to pay him a visit. However, first he made very deep snowdrifts around the lodge. Then, too, because he was an ill-natured fellow, he raised storms and a wind that cut like a knife.

When the North Wind had finished his work, he entered

the duck's lodge. He found the duck, snug and comfortable. In fact, he was singing merrily. The brave duck, upon seeing the North Wind, said, "Come, sit near the fire." Then he joked about the mild weather and laughed at the North Wind. "What's the trouble?" he asked gleefully. "Where are the icy blasts about which you boasted and with which you threatened the birds and ducks? The air is so still that the dead rushes scarcely rustle. I cannot believe that winter has arrived." As he talked, the fish duck poked the fire and added a second log.

Soon the North Wind was perplexed and awed by such a brave little duck. "No one before has ever dared to belittle my power and strength," he said to himself. "I must punish him for his boldness. No creature must ever laugh at my icy breath. I'll make him pay for his impudence." The fish duck continued to joke and be merry.

At last, the North Wind could stand neither the heat nor the duck's cheerfulness. The fire soon drove him away. The Indians claim that the North Wind's hasty departure is the reason why sometimes we have an early spring in the North land.

Forty

WHY THE CROW IS BLACK

Once upon a time when a large tribe of Indians was living along the shores of the Great Lakes, beautiful white birds came there. Some of the Indians were interested in the birds. One day, Wash-Suh-Kom called to them, "I shall paint you different colors. I do not like to have you all look alike."

Almost as soon as he had made the promise, Wash-Suh-Kom started painting the birds. He made the loon black and white and, as he painted, he gave a different color to each bird. At last, Wash-Suh-Kom was ready to paint the crow which was almost white. "I'll spot you like the loon," said the painter.

Now the crow did not want his clothes painted. He objected strongly and said, "Let me alone. I am beautiful just as I am. You must not put your brush on me!" But the Indians held the crow while Wash-Suh-Kom painted him all over. The painter said as he spread the black paint, "You are too conceited; I'll blacken you." The crow made such a fuss that he frightened the birds and even the Indians. The

189

birds flew far away and some of the Indians hurried away too, but not until the painter had finished his job.

The crow tried to catch the birds, but he was only able to catch hold of the blackbird. The crow was very angry with the birds and so he said to the blackbird, "You, at least, shall be the same color as I am." In a minute, he had rubbed some of the wet, black paint from his body all over the blackbird.

Yet the crow was still unhappy. He knew that the Indians had spoiled his fine feathers. He wanted to punish them. He decided to do it. He started north as soon as he could. There he built a fence to prevent the deer from coming to the feeding grounds where the Indians often went to shoot them.

When the braves went to the woods to hunt deer, they couldn't find any. Wash-Suh-Kom bade different birds scour the country to search for the deer, but the birds returned without having found a trace of them. Soon the Indians had no food.

Some time later, the owl, perching on a tree, saw the crow coming from the north. The crow alighted on a pine branch. He was wearing a necklace of deers' eyeballs. The owl quickly told the Indians. Then they realized that the crow knew where the deer were.

They hurried to the crow and said, "You are keeping the deer from us." The crow laughed and answered, "Well, you made me black. Now you, yourselves, will soon look black from starvation."

Wash-Suh-Kom bade the owl watch the crow's movements very closely. The owl saw the crow fly first south and then go in the opposite direction until it disappeared between two high hills or dunes.

All the Indians started to follow the crow. At last, they came to a large field with a high fence and a big gate. There they could see many deer in the field. The Indians sent several animals to get through the gate, but the crow beat them back with a club. The wolves tried first; then a wild cat attempted to get through, but the crow dealt him a blow that flattened his nose to its present shape. Then two foxes were sent. They got through the gate, for they were

191

too quick and sly for the crow. Soon they freed the deer which hurried from the field.

The crow wept at the loss of his game, but by his magic which the Indians call "medicine" he made the skins of the fleeing deer so hard that the braves' weapons could not pass through them. And so, the Indians continued to starve.

But after a while, the crow was satisfied and said, "You played a mean trick on me, but I have had my revenge by making you very hungry. From this time, you shall be able to chase the deer again; only be sure to leave the liver and the inside fat for me."

The Indians joyfully promised to do so as long as the crow lived. Then their young braves hurried to the woods. There they got plenty of venison. Even to this day, the Indians, because of their promise, leave the guts and fat for the crows.

Forty-one

THE EAGLE

The birds met together one day for a council. Wood-peckers, larks, blue jays, robins, sparrows, and a gray linnet were among the first to arrive. An owl came along. The hawks, geese, and an eagle reached the meeting place last. The whole place was busy and noisy.

These birds at the council acted very much like people. They strutted, boasted, and quarrelled. Some of them were very proud of their splendid voices; others boasted of their beautiful plumage. The owl blinked and said, "Well, I may not be beautiful, but I can see in the dark far better than any of the rest of you." A few boasted of their strength. The geese claimed that they could fly a long distance. At last, the skylark piped up, "I feel sure that I can fly the highest. Although I build my home on the ground, I sing as I fly far up in the sky. People hear my song when I am so high that they cannot see me." Thus, the birds talked and argued for hours. Each one was sure that he could fly the highest.

Finally, it seemed that only a contest would settle the dispute. The council decided to give a prize to the bird that

could fly higher than the others. So the contest began. Some of the birds flew up very swiftly, but they soon became tired. Some were slower, but they were stronger and could stay in the air longer. Others flew quite close to the earth. The eagle, with its broad wings, flew beyond them all. He soared away up through the clouds. But just at the moment when the eagle was ready to claim the victory, a gray linnet claimed the prize too. The gray linnet is a very small bird. During the contest, when no one was looking, it had perched on the eagle's back. There it took a free ride. Of course, because it was fresh and not tired, the gray linnet was then able to fly to the top of the sky.

But the council finally gave the prize to the eagle. That bird had not only gone nearer to the sun than any of the larger birds, but it had also carried the linnet on its back. The birds all agreed that the decision was fair.

Since that time, Indian warriors have adorned themselves with the eagle's feathers. Its feathers are the greatest mark of honor that an Indian can wear.

194

Forty-two

WHY THE ROBIN HAS A RED BREAST

Many years ago in the cold Northland, there was a great blazing fire. In fact, it was the only fire in all the world. All day and all night, Scarface, an Indian hunter, and his little son, Wolf Tail, tended the fire and kept it burning brightly. Many animals crept near the fire to warm their feet. The rabbits, limping with half-numb legs over the frozen ground in search of food, rejoiced to thaw their frozen toes in the warmth of the blaze. From great distances, the Indians came for live coals that they might cook their food. Both the Indians and the animals were thankful for the fire.

One day, Scarface became very ill. He lay suffering with such chills and fever that he could no longer care for the fire. Wolf Tail, day after day, and night after night, took care of his sick father and tended the fire faithfully. To keep it burning, he would rush off to the woods for twigs and sticks, and then hurry back to toss them upon the embers. He had no time for sleep. But at last, he became too tired to keep his eyes open any longer. While he was watching one night in front of the fire, his head began to nod and he fell asleep on the ground.

Now at this same time in the deep woods of the Northland there lived a mean, white bear. For days, he had watched the fire as he walked about among the dense pines. He hated all warm things. He wanted to put out the fire, but he didn't dare go near it for he was afraid of the hunter's arrows. When the bear saw that Wolf Tail had fallen asleep, he smiled broadly and began to step softly nearer and nearer the fire.

"Now this is my chance! How I have longed to put out that fire!" he said happily.

Then he jumped upon the burning sticks with his big, wet feet and trampled the flaming pieces into the snow. He tramped back and forth until not a spark seemed to be left. Then he went back to his cave in the woods, quite satisfied, for he was sure that the fire was dead.

While the mean, white bear was putting out the fire, a little robin sat in the hemlock tree watching. When she saw the bear's bad deed, she was sorry. She realized how much suffering this act would cause. She hurriedly flew down to the ground to the spot where the fire had been. What do you suppose she saw? Yes, there was a tiny spark and one red coal. The little robin began hopping about and fanning the spark with her wings to make it burn brighter. Soon the red coal began to crackle and in a short time, the twigs and branches were burning as brightly as ever. As the flame shot higher and higher, it scorched the poor robin's breast; the brave, little bird didn't mind, for she was happy to have saved the fire.

When the flames were again leaping toward the sky, Wolf Tail awoke. The old, white bear was terribly angry that his effort was a failure. He growled and growled. The robin had gone back to her place in the hemlock tree. When she looked down where the flames had burned her breast, she discovered that her feathers were no longer the color of her body. Her breast had been changed to a beautiful golden red. The Indians love the robin. They claim that because of her thoughtfulness for others and her brave act, she received the lovely red breast.

Forty-three

THE FIRST WOODPECKER

Long and long ago, Manabozho, the Great Spirit, often walked up and down the earth. He listened to the troubles of the Chippewas and helped those that were hungry, cold, and sick, for the Great Spirit loved all his people and liked to have them well and happy.

One day, he went to a wigwam where a squaw lived all alone. She was building a fire near the wigwam when Manabozho approached it. This woman looked attractive in her black dress, gay red cap, and big white apron as she fanned the flame over the open fire.

Now because Manabozho could use magic and had supernatural power, he could change himself into any form he wished. This time, he chose to look like a very old man with thick, snow-white hair and a long beard. His face was wrinkled and his body seemed weak and thin. Of course, when Manabozho appeared at the doorway, the squaw did not recognize him. In fact, she had lived alone so long that she was not interested in anyone except herself, and scarcely noticed the old man.

"Have mercy upon me, for I am very hungry. I have fasted for many days," said Manabozho weakly. "Please give me some food. Oh, I must sit down, for I cannot stand any longer." Trembling and exhausted, Manabozho seated himself by the fire.

Then the squaw got maize that had been pounded into meal. She took a small portion of it, made a tiny cake, and put it on the fire. As soon as she had finished, she turned to the old man and said, "You may have the cake if you will wait until it is baked."

"Oh, thank you," exclaimed the old man. "I will gladly wait, for I am very hungry."

A little later, the squaw went over to the fire to look at the cake. Imagine her surprise! The cake was a large one. "I thought it would be a little one," she said to herself. "I will not give him such a big cake." She put the cake away in her cupboard. Then she called to the old man and said, "I shall have to bake another cake. You may have it, if you care to wait until it is baked."

"I will wait," said Manabozho again.

Then the squaw took a still smaller portion of meal and stirred up another cake. When that cake was baked it was even bigger than the first one. As soon as the squaw saw it, she was very happy and exclaimed, "This cake is so large that I shall keep it for the Ceremonial Feast." Then, turning to her guest, she said, "I will not give you this cake, but if you will wait, I will bake you another one."

"I will wait," replied Manabozho.

This time, the squaw took even less meal than she had used previously. The amount would scarcely cover the palm of her hand. Yet when she took this cake from the oven, it was the largest one that she had ever baked.

The squaw was puzzled! She couldn't understand why

the last cake should be so very large. Of course, she did not realize that it was Manabozho's magic that had made each cake larger than the one that she had baked previously.

"Well, I shall not be such a fool to give away the largest cake I've ever baked!" she concluded. Then she turned to Manabozho and said, "I have no food for a beggar. Go find it in the forest. You can find food in the bark of the trees and in the roots of the plants. Don't trouble me any longer!"

Manabozho was indignant when he heard the squaw's words. Rising to his feet, he said with great earnestness, "A squaw should be good and kind, but you are cruel, selfish, and greedy. You shall no longer be a squaw and live in a wigwam. Henceforth, you must go out into the forest and hunt for your food in the bark of trees."

Then the Great Spirit stamped his foot and snapped his fingers. The squaw grew smaller and smaller every minute. At last, she looked like a small bird. Manabozho changed her black dress to glossy black feathers and the white apron to white feathers to cover the under-part of her body. Then he gave her a bonnet of red feathers to cover her head and neck. Soon black wings sprouted on each side of her body. Immediately, with a flutter of her wings, she rose from the ground and flew away to the woods.

Ever since, she has lived in the forest. All day long, she runs up and down the trunks of trees and dead tree trunks in search of food. Her stiff, spiny tail feathers enable her to climb or rest on a tree's trunk while she pecks and drills with her chisel-like beak into the hard bark for insects.

If you listen, you can still hear that selfish old squaw tap, tap, tap. Today we call her the red-headed woodpecker.

HOW I COLLECTED THE LEGENDS

My friendship with the Chippewas began a long time ago when my father was pastor of the Methodist Church at Charlevoix, Michigan. Connected with this parish was an Indian Mission, built in 1844, and known as Greensky Hill. In those days, several hundred Indian families attended this small church of finely hewn logs. It was set in a dense grove somberly guarded by towering pine and spruce trees, and with a cemetery adjacent to it. My father directed the work of the four local Indian preachers who talked to the congregation in their native tongue.

The Indians had petty jealousies, slights, and grievances which they did not hesitate to bring to their pastor. My father was the arbiter when trouble arose. Since the Indians frequently came to our home, I became interested in them. Because of their love and admiration for my father, the Indians grew to like his family, too.

At different times we employed Indian women in our home. I never mentioned a legend until I had known these women for a long time, for I knew that my request would be denied. Even today the Chippewas will tell their legends only to those whom they greatly esteem. To gain their confidence is a real hurdle.

On a cool morning in early June, when I chanced to walk along the beach, I saw that someone had started a fire a short distance away. As I approached it, I noticed that an Indian woman, whom I had met at the Mission, was having a weiner roast for her two small sons. Offering them some candy bars I asked if I might share her fire for a few minutes. She consented. After the boys had finished their breakfast, they coaxed their mother for some stories. I listened carefully and jotted down my first two legends: "Why the Rabbit Has Long Ears" and "Why the Raccoon Has Rings on Its Tail." Later, I persuaded Dan McSauba, the grandson of Chief McSauba, our postman, to tell me about "Glooskap's Gifts to the Three Seekers." At the August Indian Camp Meeting, to which the Indians from all over Michigan and Wisconsin came, I heard one of the Indian preachers tell about

"The Creation of the World" and "The Origin of the Races." While picnicking on the shore of Susan Lake with an Indian girl, I admired the water lilies and the towering pines and said, "I wish I knew stories about them. Do you happen to know any?" She smiled and after considerable coaxing related "The Star Maiden." I noticed that she had been admiring a hat I was wearing. I finally said, "I believe Mary would tell me the legend about the pine tree. If she does, I'll give her this hat." "Don't give it to her. I want it," Lizzie said sharply and, without further hesitation, recalled "Why the Pine Trees Weep."

Not all of the stories came so easily. Often I worked six weeks to get a complete legend. A pound of bacon, a basket of groceries, or a pretty house dress often helped the aged squaws to recall legends they said they had completely forgotten or could remember only in part.

My experiences with the Chippewas were amusing, sometimes irritating and disappointing, but never dull. To induce other Indians to tell one of their legends I took them for their first ride in an automobile, bought tickets for them to go to Harbor Springs on the *Manitou*, provided a Christmas tree and presents for their children, sent flowers and food when they were sick, attended the funerals of their loved ones, and gave money to those who were particularly hard pressed.

It is a loss to American literature that so much of the legendary history of the Chippewas has gone beyond hope of recovery. For as each aged Indian has passed away, some bit of history or tradition known perhaps only to him has been lost forever. Since these tales constitute their only history, it is to be regretted that more of these legends cannot be collected and preserved as our cultural heritage from the first Americans.

ANSWER TO PICTURE WRITING

Chief McSauba calls a council. The chiefs come together. Chief McSauba talks to the Indians. He tells them to stop fighting. They smoke the peace pipe. The Indians leave as friends.

SISTERS BY CHOICE

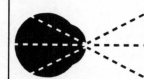

This Large Print Book carries the
Seal of Approval of N.A.V.H.

SISTERS BY CHOICE

SUSAN MALLERY

THORNDIKE PRESS
A part of Gale, a Cengage Company

LIBRARY OF CONGRESS CIP DATA ON FILE.
CATALOGUING IN PUBLICATION FOR THIS BOOK
IS AVAILABLE FROM THE LIBRARY OF CONGRESS

ISBN-13: 978-1-4328-7624-1 (hardcover alk. paper)

Published in 2020 by arrangement with Harlequin Books S.A.

Printed in Mexico
Print Number: 01   Print Year: 2020

For Tarryn — I know you love my
Blackberry Island books so I'm thrilled
to be able to dedicate this one to you.
I think you're going to enjoy meeting
Sophie and Kristine and Heather.
And, okay, even Amber.
I hope you have as much fun reading
this book as I had writing it!